An Unexpected Reality

An Unexpected Reality

By

Clara Matson

Cover picture: ID 74138911 © Michael Gray | Dreamstime.com

Cover design: Bethany Matson

Acknowledgement

I want to thank all those whose experiences with cancer helped me create this book. You know who you are. I couldn't have done it without you.

Dedication

To Don, who assures me that taking time out
to write isn't a waste of time.

Table of Contents

Chapter 1 Dreams

I stand by the ocean on an outcrop of rock. The waves crash against it, splashing my feet and wetting the hem of my jeans. The air, heavy with the feel and smell of the ocean and all that lives there, swirls around me–embracing me. My eyes search the horizon for something; I don't know what. It's one of those things which lingers in the back of your mind, taunting you with its existence, but never giving you the gift of a hint.

A voice in the distance pulls at me, but I'm not ready to leave. I try to ignore it, but its insistent call forces me away from my search of the horizon. The voice becomes clearer now, and I understand that it's calling my name.

"Jenn, Jenn," it calls. I tear myself away from the ocean and turn toward the voice. "Jenn… Jennifer," it says in a sing-songy way. It's my mother.

Slowly and painfully, I open my eyes and look around. My world has transformed from the beckoning ocean to my bedroom. The roar of the waves is now just the slow tick of the clock on my nightstand. The breeze, which breathed life into me, has been replaced with warm, stuffy, morning air.

My mother is stroking my arm, "Come on, Honey. Your appointment is in an hour." Today is the day I am finally going to get some answers–at least, I hope.

I slowly get out of bed and run my fingers through my hair. With a little brushing I think it will be presentable enough. I don't have the energy for a shower. I smell my underarms and look at my reflection in the mirror.

"Ravishing," I mutter sarcastically. I run my hands down my face pulling at my cheeks till my eyes are stretched out enough that I can see the insides of my bottom lids. My eyes are completely bloodshot. I groan and sweep my hair up into a messy bun. The underwear I slip into is loose and threatens to fall off my hips. My figure has finally caught up to my appetite.

After I dress, I go to the kitchen and cringe at the sight of the table. Horrible memories of breakfast the day before come flooding back. I remember how the sight of the food Mom had laid out for me made my stomach roil with disgust. I knew I needed to eat something, so I forced myself to sit and take a few bites of buttered toast and four grapes–the red kind. I like those the best. It didn't take much to make me feel full, but I still managed to chug down my glass of orange juice, to please Mom. Without warning, all the food I'd eaten came back up. Orange juice splashed all over the table, soaking the place mats. I looked at Mom and saw the stunned look of concern on her face. I realized then that she had just witnessed for the first time the reason why I've been so worried. In seconds she was at my side with a washcloth to wipe my face. She rubbed my arm and repeatedly said, "It's ok, baby. It's ok."

"This is why I wanted to come home," I said between mini gags. "I was afraid that one day I would throw up in front of everyone in the cafeteria." Because of my inability to keep food down and my growing weakness and fears, I knew I wouldn't be able to keep up with my studies. So, mid-semester I came home, leaving behind my college life.

Mom jingles the car keys bringing me back to the present. She stands at the door to the garage smiling and asks, "Are you ready?"

I nod, and in no time, we're in the car heading to my appointment. As we drive, it begins to rain. I watch as large drops of water splash onto the road turning the asphalt dark black.

My head rests against the window, dry on my side of the glass, and I think of how my head is less than a half an inch away from the world of wetness on the other side.

My head bobs with the movement of the car and a thought creeps into my brain, *I'm going to miss the feel of rain on my skin.* The thought startles me. I quickly push it away.

We pull up under the porte-cochere and park. I'm disappointed because I so wanted to feel the rain. Mom jumps out, trying to reach my side of the car before I get out. I already have one leg out but am grateful for her assistance after that. She hands the keys to the valet and guides me into the Digestive Health Center. We walk to the front desk where they get me checked in, strap two bands to my wrist and direct us to the waiting room where we sit and wait. I put my head on my mom's shoulder searching for some comfort. Finally, they call my name. The nurse leads us through a set of large white doors into the back area. It reminds me a lot of a small emergency room. She shows us to a small alcove of a room. The open side has only a curtain for privacy. She directs me to sit on the gurney enveloped in white sheets and asks me my name.

"Jennifer Cooper," I respond.

"Good answer," she replies with a chuckle as she scans my wrist bands, medication bottles, and charts.

I lose interest in what she's doing until I hear my mom talk. I look up as she says, "Yes, I'm Sandra Cooper, her mother." Her voice sounds thick as if she were talking through a mouthful of mush and it hits me how hard this must be for her. She's already walked down a similar path, years ago with my dad. Now, long after my memories of him have been lost along with my baby teeth and my stuffed rabbit, she must walk this path again with me. It seems so unfair.

The nurse pulls me from my thoughts by asking more questions. She hands me a "see more buns" gown, as my sister, Maggie calls it, and pulls the curtain closed behind her to give me some privacy to change. As I pull off my clothes, I hear a sharp gasp from my mother. I glance at her and see tears welling in her eyes as she scans my emaciated body. I shrug my shoulders and give her an apologetic look. I don't know what else to do.

When I have the gown secure, the nurse returns and adeptly inserts an IV into my arm. I watch transfixed as the liquid drips from the bag of saline, runs down the tube and into my arm. She puts an injection into a port midway down the tube. The liquid blends with the saline and disappears into my body. Within moments, my head starts to feel heavy, and sleep overtakes me.

Once again, I'm standing on the outcrop of rock. The waves crash against it, splashing my feet and wetting the hem of my skirt. *A skirt?* I wonder, *Why am I wearing a full-length skirt?* My thoughts are pulled away from the incongruency by the fresh air. It speaks to me of life as it swirls around me, enveloping me. My eyes search the horizon for something. I don't know what – no, wait, I do. I remember now. I'm waiting for a ship, but I'm not sure why. I feel something rub my arm. I look down but all I see is a crisp white blouse. Its long sleeves billow out at the shoulder and taper down to a straight sleeve at the forearm. I put my hand to my throat and finger the brooch pinned to the neck of the high collar. There are ruffles running down the front of the blouse. I run my hand down them, fascinated by the play of motion my hand creates. I laugh at how ridiculous I must look and at how out of character this outfit is for me. I would never be caught dead wearing anything like this. It must be Halloween.

I climb down from the rocks and walk along the beach, the whole time watching the waves crashing against my feet. I'm wearing old fashioned shoes. I'd seen some like them on the cover of an old book I'd read years ago. The name of these types of shoes was also the title of the book. I think for a few minutes, looking at the buttons that run up the side of the shoes then recall, "*High Button Shoes*." That was the name of the book and that's the kind of shoes I'm wearing. A longing to feel the cool sand on my feet and the frothy waves crashing against my skin becomes powerful, so I sit on a log and begin to unbutton my shoes. As I do so, I feel that rubbing again and hear someone say my name. It is becoming more insistent. Suddenly, I feel someone shove me and I fall off the log and into the hospital bed at the Digestive Health Center. I open my eyes and see Mom's relieved face looking down at me.

Mom sighs and says, "You had me worried when you wouldn't wake up."

"I was about ready to call the doc," the nurse interjects.

"I was having a strange dream," I say, which causes the nurse to give my mom a puzzled look. "What?" I ask looking from Mom to the nurse then back again.

"Well," the nurse begins, measuring her words with care. "This kind of anesthesia causes amnesia. You shouldn't have dreamed, let alone remembered it. Strange," she says and writes something in my chart and leaves. Mom stands vigil at my side, smiling at me and rubbing my arm. I can't stand the sight of the intense worry behind that smile and turn away, trying to concentrate instead on the sounds filtering in from the other curtained rooms.

All too soon, the doctor comes in and stands on the opposite side of the bed from Mom. He's very handsome, and I'm not sure, but it seems Mom's pretty smitten with him. She can't take her eyes off him. He *is* very dreamy in an old-enough-to-be-my-dad kind of way, but I guess he is the right age for Mom.

After staring at Mom for what seems like a long time, he introduces himself. "H... hi, erm…hello. I'm Dr. Scott Pearson," he stammers. Mom takes his extended hand, and they shake and keep shaking. They can't stop looking at each other. I've always thought Mom was beautiful in a matronly kind of way and looks young enough to be my older sister, but the way he's looking at her, forces me to see her in a new light. I tilt my head as I squint away the wrinkles at the corners of her eyes and try to imagine her twenty years younger.

Finally, the doctor turns to me and says, "Well, we've got some good news and some bad news." I nod encouragingly at him. "The bad news is," he pauses, gathering his courage, "you have stomach cancer." Mom gasps and tries in vain to stifle a sob which extracts a sympathetic look from the doctor. He reaches over and puts a comforting hand on her arm.

Turning back to me, he braces himself for my reaction. "Well, that explains a lot," I say, which elicits a soft chuckle from the doctor. "I'm just grateful to finally have some answers. So, what's the good news?"

"Well, it looks like we caught it soon enough that there's a good chance of beating this thing. And since you're young – what are you, seventeen?" he asks.

Irritated that he's taking me for a high schooler, I correct him, "I'm twenty."

"Oh," he says and looks at my chart presumably to check my age – then continues what he'd started to say, "Well you're in good health, other than the cancer, so your prognosis is very promising."

Dr. Pearson lays his laptop on the bed and opens it. Scrolling through my chart he opens the pictures of my insides and shows us what my stomach looks like. I must say it doesn't look pretty even with the cancer mucking it all up. He then gives Mom the name and contact information for a local oncologist, Dr. Wilson Milward, who specializes in stomach cancer. He explains that someone from Dr. Milward's office will be contacting me in a day or two to set up an appointment for a consultation. Mom nods and sniffles, giving the doctor an adorable smile.

When he hands her his card, he clasps her hand in both of his and says, "If you need *anything*, just give me a call."

Wait a minute, I think. *This doctor is hitting on my mother at the same time as he's giving me the bad news. Is that even ethical?* At first, I'm irritated, but then as I watch them interact, I realize my mom's been alone for a long time. It's time she has someone in her life who makes her happy. Besides if this cancer thing goes south, she'll have someone besides Maggie to comfort her.

I smile at her when he leaves and say, "Why, Sandy, I believe you have an admirer."

"What?" she says looking somewhere between sheepish and shocked.

While Mom is distracted with the paperwork the nurse hands her, I dress quickly. I check my phone and see Maggie has texted at least five times, no doubt unable to concentrate on her job. I also see that Hunter left a message. My heart lurches when I see it.

How do I tell him that his girlfriend has cancer? I wonder. *I wouldn't blame him if he dumped me.* I turn off the screen and pocket my phone when Mom returns from returning the paperwork to the nurse's desk.

"Ready?" she asks. I nod and we walk toward the exit. Before we make it to the door, *Dr. Hunky* comes to bid us farewell.

"Remember, Sandy, if you need anything, please give me a call. I know how difficult this can be," he says, gently squeezing her upper arm. I try in vain to stifle my grin but am unsuccessful, so I quickly turn and leave. Like a couple of teenage girls at the mall Mom and I giggle our way to the car. It's not until I feel my phone vibrate and see that my younger sister Maggie has texted yet again, that I remember the bad news Dr. Hunky had given us just a few minutes before. Once we're settled in the car, I shoot Maggie a text to let her know we're on our way home.

As we turn onto our street, I see Maggie's car in the driveway and a sinking feeling fills my belly. I don't want to tell her. I don't want to say the "C" word in conjunction with my name, but it's part of who I am now, part of my reality. I decide to just do it and get it over with, like ripping off the proverbial bandage.

We walk in the door and find Maggie at the table staring off into space, automatically popping M&M's from the bowl in front of her into her mouth. The glass of diet cola next to the bowl stands untouched. Our approach pulls her from her thoughts. She stands and anxiously asks, "Well? What did the doctor say?" Mom's choked sob is all Maggie needs to know it's bad. "Is it c-cancer?" she asks, her eyes wide with fear. Mom nods. Maggie slumps back into her chair looking shaken.

Suddenly, I feel perturbed by all this drama on my behalf and say, "Alright, you two, that's enough! It's not like I'm dying right now. In fact, Dr. Pearson said with treatments I could live a long healthy life." It wasn't exactly what he said, but I hope my additions will be enough to snap them out of their *boohooing.* "Hey," I continue, "I'm in the mood for a milkshake." In reality, I know I probably won't be able to keep it down. They look at me as if seeing me for the first time.

"Yes," Mom says, brightening a bit as she wipes a tear from her cheek.

Maggie hugs me and whispers, "I love you, Sis." A lump forms in my throat and tears threaten to give away my true feelings.

I push her away, playfully slug her in the shoulder, and say with a cheeky grin, "Aww, you big weenie!" She looks at me shocked, and I sling my arm around her shoulder and say, "First one to the car gets shotgun!" With every bit of energy I can muster, I start jogging toward the car. At first, I don't hear anything behind me, but before long, I hear Maggie squeal and quickly run up from behind. And the race is on.

Chapter 2 Old Friends

That night as I lie in bed, I hear Mom in the room next door quietly crying. For the first time, the weight of my diagnosis presses in on me as if the six-foot bookshelf next to my bed has crashed down on me, mercilessly crushing me into my bed. I can hardly breathe. A sob forces its way from my chest and tears course down my cheeks.

I feel the need to run, to get away, to be anywhere but here. Then I realize the reality. My disease will follow me wherever I go. I remember the visualization exercises my roommate and I would do right before a test to help us relax. It gives me the idea that maybe there is a place I can go, in my mind, that doesn't include cancer. I go through the usual images I would use, but none of them feel right. Then my mind finds itself remembering the scene from my dreams, the feel of the ocean breeze caressing my face, the spray of the water and smell of life all around me.

Yes, I think, *I want to be there.* I force my mind to go there, to sit on the beach and to imagine that ship breaching the horizon. My heart begins to flutter with excitement, and I wonder if my thinking about it will cause me to dream about it. I lie there with my eyes closed, thinking about my ocean perch, for what feels like at least an hour until finally my body accepts the sleep it so desperately wants and needs.

I'm standing on the outcrop of rock again. The ship is now anchored just offshore. Its white sails billow on the breeze, the same breeze which brings me the sounds of wood creaking and sails snapping. Every so often I catch shouts rising up over the crash of the waves. Some of them are audible like "bulkhead," "hoist," and "port bow." I can see men scampering along the rigging helping to take in the sails. A dinghy is being lowered over the side with a man aboard. It splashes into the water, and for a moment I fear the man will topple out. But the craft quickly rights itself and he commences to row toward shore–toward me.

I shade my eyes with my hand trying to get a better look at the man in the dinghy. All I can tell is that he's tall and he's wearing a dark blue uniform of some type. As the dinghy draws nearer, a flutter of nervousness develops in my stomach.

Why am I so nervous? I wonder. With no real answer, I scramble down from my perch to wait. I watch and pace, watch and pace until I can hardly stand it anymore. I think of running away, but something compels me to stay. I jump when the dinghy's weight causes the sand to make a squelching sound as it reaches the shore. The man disembarks, turns, and smiles the most winning smile I've ever seen, and my heart does a flip. There's something familiar about his smile, but I can't figure it out. It feels as if it's a smile from a long-forgotten dream.

His frame is lean and muscular, and his face, weathered, sporting unkempt facial hair. It has a red tint to it and frames his handsome smile charmingly. When he removes his cap, locks of auburn, curly hair tumble down onto his brow and around the nape of his neck. Although he's in great need of some grooming, his eyes are kind, and they twinkle when he looks at me. A sigh escapes my lips when I look at them. They're brown and remind me of almonds floating in sweet cream.

Whoa! Wait! Did I just sigh? I think. It's then I realize he's holding out his hand. I stare at it for a moment, stunned to see it there. No. Stunned by the whole experience. *It all feels so real yet how could that be? It's only a dream.* I think. I narrow my eyes and fix him with a suspicious look, and he withdraws his hand.

His smile turns sad, and he says, "I guess I was expecting too much to think you would remember me."

"Remember you?" I say, afraid to reveal how familiar he seems. "Have we met?"

"Yes," his face hopeful, "many years ago…in another life."

"In another life?"

"Well, sort of," he says getting flustered, "it's hard to explain."

"Oh," I reply, suddenly feeling awkward. It all seems so strange. I take a steading breath and say, "So...*Old Friend*, what's your name?"

His grin returns. He bows and says, "Jack Callaghan, at your service."

Dang! I think as my heart does another of those stupid, uncontrollable flips. Startled by my feelings, I turn and stroll down the beach. Jack falls in step next to me and we walk companionably for quite a while before we speak.

"Um...I guess I should introduce myself," I say.

"Oh, I know your name," he says.

"Oh, really?" I say, fixing him with a skeptical look.

"Yes, remember we're old friends," he begins with mounting excitement. "Your name is Jennifer Cooper and you've been a part of my life for over 150 years. You were a strength to me when I needed you most, and I'm here to help you through your ordeal with cancer." The mention of cancer startles me, partly because I'm not used to hearing the disease in conjunction with my name, but also because he knows.

How does he know? I wonder, *I haven't told anyone but Maggie.*

Freaked out, I stop, stare at him, and ask, "How did you know that? Are you some kind of stalker?"

"Oh, I'm so sorry. I didn't mean to frighten you," he says. He interlaces his fingers, twiddling his thumbs, looking nervous. "Would you like me to leave?" he asks.

I think the smart thing would be to send him away, but something long dormant awakens in me and I can't bring myself to do it. Then I remind myself this is just a dream, anyway, and that he can't truly hurt me. I look down at the sand and say with a smile, "No, no you can stay. Just don't get creepy again, Okay?"

His dazzling smile spreads across his face, and he says, "Agreed."

We continue walking again. After a few yards, I open my mouth to say something and all that comes out is a buzzing noise. I stop and shake my head and try again. Once again, the buzzing noise comes from my mouth. I look around and everything, including Jack, becomes watery and pale. All goes black but the buzzing continues. I open my eyes and I'm in my room. The morning sunlight pours through the window creating a kite shaped square on the floor. The sound of my alarm clock stabs my head and stomach with shots of adrenaline. I groan, roll over, and slap the snooze button. I had forgotten to turn the alarm off the night before.

I roll onto my back and stare at the ceiling contemplating my future, or what little I may have, and wonder what I should do. I grab my phone from my nightstand and start googling stomach cancer. Each possible treatment jabs me in the chest until I feel as if I'm going to vomit. I turn off my phone, roll over, bury my face in my pillow, and let loose the scream that has been building inside me for the last twenty-four hours.

Tears flow unchecked and thoughts of *Why me?* whirl in a wicked dance around my brain. Then thoughts that the doctor could be mistaken, partner with the *Why me?* thoughts until they're doing an even wilder jig, spinning out of control. I feel like my head will split open any moment, and all those thoughts will spill out taking on a life of their own, dancing around my room whooping and howling. I clamp my hands around my head and squeeze. That's when it hits me that the doctor couldn't be mistaken. I'd seen the scans myself. I'd felt the symptoms and I knew. I have stomach cancer.

Just then my phone rings and I jump. Looking at the caller ID, I don't recognize the number. At first, I consider rejecting the call, but then realize it might be the oncologist's office calling. "Hello?" I say.

"Hello," says an all-too-perky voice, "This is April from Dr. Milward's office. Is this Jennifer?"

"Yes," I confirm.

"Great. We received a referral from Dr. Pearson for you. Is that correct?"

"Yes."

"Great,"

Again with the Great, I think.

"Well," she continues, "we can set up an appointment for you on Friday. Do you have any particular time you'd like to come in?"

Never, I think, but then reply, "No, anytime would be fine."

"Great, does 10:30 sound good to you?"

"Yeah," I deadpan.

"Great, please arrive fifteen minutes early to fill out the new patient forms."

"Ok."

"Great, we're looking forward to working with you. Have a nice day and we'll see you on Friday. Bye-bye." Click.

Great? Maybe her life is great but not the patients she's calling. Have a nice day? Looking forward to working with me? What is wrong with that woman? I think for a while and then realize Friday is just three days away.

I roll over and bury my face once more in my already wet pillow and mutter, "I can't do this." As I replay the conversation with April about my upcoming appointment, my heart thumps so hard it feels as if it might beat right out of my chest. I start to breathe heavily and rapidly, and I feel as if I might pass out, then a thought slowly creeps in that maybe it would be better if I just died now. It would be easier for everyone. The image of Mom and Maggie weeping over my closed casket startles me. *Why is it closed? Is it because I blew my face off and the sight of it is just too disturbing?* The morbidity of my thoughts repulses me.

I lie in my bed and watch the kite shape of light turn into a rectangle and slowly slide across my floor toward me. As I try to block all thoughts out of my mind, a melody begins to tickle my consciousness. It takes me a few minutes to recognize it, but as the words start filtering into my memory, I realize it's from years ago when we used to go to church before Dad died. The song is about how to pray.

Prayer. It's been so long since I've prayed. I'm not sure I know how to anymore, I think. I debate for some time whether I should do it or not when I finally come to the conclusion it's worth a try. The worst that could happen is sore knees.

I slide out of my bed and kneel beside it. I lean face first into my bedding feeling very much like a pig at a trough of food.

Piggies at a trough, I think, and chuckle at the memory of Dad calling Maggie and me that when he'd pray with us. I rack my brain trying to remember the words to the song. The beginning part comes to me. We sang about closing our eyes and bowing our heads. *But how do I start talking to God?* I wonder. I experiment with a few options. "Hey God? Yo God? Hey you?" None of them sound right. Just then, I remember something I'd heard about God being our father and that we should talk to him as if he is our earthly father. I like this idea, so that's how I begin.

I clasp my hands together, bow my head, and start whispering. "Dear Father," I begin, "Do you know that I have cancer? Well, of course you do. You're God, and you know everything." I softly chuckle then continue. "Well, I don't want to die. I know they say there's a good chance they can cure this, but I'm not so sure and I'm scared." Just then, a warm feeling comes over me as if someone has wrapped me in a warm blanket and I feel like everything will be alright. I pray a few more minutes about Hunter, Mom, and Maggie, and I feel a lot calmer about them. Then I pray about those dreams I've been having, and I get the impression that God...or...Father has blessed me with something very special. This makes me feel a lot better about the dreams and Jack. I decide to give him a chance and just enjoy the experience.

Suddenly, I realize I don't know how to finish the prayer, but then an image pops into my mind of a fun grandma-like lady teaching a group of us kids the words to that song. As clear as if it were in front of me at that very moment, I can remember the poster she displayed with words and pictures on it to help us learn the song. With a smile, I finish my prayer by saying the words from the poster, "In Jesus name, Amen."

When I'm finished, I crawl back in bed and bask in the warm, peaceful feelings I've received from my prayer. After a few minutes I hear a gentle knock on my door. "Come in," I call.

The door slowly creaks open a crack, and I see a wedge of Maggie's face smashed up against the door frame. "Can I come in?" she asks timidly.

"Of course," I say. In a flash she is climbing into bed with me, transporting me to the time when we were little girls giggling under the covers. We talk about everything under the sun except my disease. It feels almost like a carefully coordinated dance around a very obvious, very large elephant in the fine China department of a Bed Bath and Beyond. A short time later, Mom comes in and sits on the edge of the bed. Before long we're all laughing as if nothing is any different about our existence. It puzzles me, but I don't want to break this magic spell.

"Remember those dolls we used to have? The ones that talked and we used to drive the neighbor boys crazy with them?" Maggie asks.

"Yes! I loved those dolls. Whatever happened to them?" I ask.

"I ran into Les last month at the grocery store, and he told me the whole story of how those dolls came to be missing," Maggie continues.

"No, it was Les?"

"And Kyle. I guess we'd left them at their house one day when their parents weren't home and Les and Kyle set them up in their backyard and used them for target practice," Maggie continues.

"What? Those monsters!" I screech.

"Just wait, it gets worse. They knew they had to dispose of the evidence, so they threw them over the fence into the neighbor's pool. About two hours later they came flying back over the fence into their yard with their motors cut out and the remains of their bodies tied together."

"No way! What did they do then?"

"Oh, just wait. They buried them in the flowerbed in their backyard and figured they'd gotten away with the dastardly deed. But when their parents got home, their little brother, Sammy, remember him?" I nod. "He squealed on them and so their parents made them exhume the bodies."

"I always liked that kid," I say. Suddenly, I realize Mom isn't reacting in any way. I turn to her and say, "Did you know about this?"

She looks down at her blouse and begins straightening the gathers.

"Mo-om…tell the truth," I needle.

"Well, you two were driving *me* crazy with those dolls. I'd regretted buying them for you from the first day, but you both loved them so much…so…well…I was the one who left them at their house," she confessed.

"On purpose?" Maggie asks, disbelieving.

"I had no idea they would do all of that to them. I was just looking for a short respite from that incessant chatter. I must confess when I heard what they'd done I…I…well, I wasn't disappointed."

"What!" Maggie and I bellow.

"Why are we just now hearing about this?" I ask.

She looks at her blouse again and smooths it straight, adding, without meeting our eyes, "I paid them to keep it quiet. I guess I'm going to have to go and demand my money back."

This is more than we can take, and we laugh till tears pour down our cheeks. I laugh so hard I can barely catch my breath, then something changes. I look at Maggie, but she's no longer laughing but crying. She grabs me and pulls me close. "I'm so scared, Jenn. Please don't leave us, *please*," she begs.

I don't know what to say, so I just hold her as tight as I can, relieved the elephant is finally out in the open. Mom joins us then and our laughter-filled room turns to a pool of tears.

We lie there and cry until we run out of tears. Mom is the first to let go. "Why don't I go make us some pancakes?" she says, then asks, "Is that something you think you can keep down?"

I shrug my shoulders and say, "We won't know until we try." Mom nods and leaves.

I hear my phone vibrate and intuitively know it's Hunter again. I feel as if ice water shoots through me. I groan, hating myself for putting him off this long. I show Maggie the screen.

"Oh, boy," she says. The phone continues to ring. I'm stuck in my indecision. I know he's probably worried. I know I must tell him sometime soon. On the fourth ring I realize I can't put this off any longer and answer the call.

"Hi, Hunter," I say. Maggie nods and starts to get up, but I grab her and pull her back down. I put the phone between us so she can hear and hopefully coach me through it. She snuggles close.

"Hey, you answered! I was beginning to think you were ghosting me. How's my girl?" he asks.

"Well, I've had better days," I say.

"And those are the ones you've spent with me. Right?" he jokes. I chuckle, then his tone turns serious. "No, really. When are you coming back? I miss you."

I sigh and take a deep breath and blurt, "I won't be back for a long time. Hunter, I have cancer."

The other end is silent for several moments and I'm beginning to think we've been disconnected when he says, "This better not be some kind of sadistic joke."

"I wish it was," I say, my voice catching with emotion.

He blows out his breath and stumbles for something to say.

I can just imagine him rubbing his forehead the way he always does when he's unsure of himself. Thinking of him brings a tender smile to my face, and I say, "Hunter, I know this is a lot to process. I'm still trying to process it myself. Why don't you take a couple of days to think about it and we can talk again on the weekend?"

"Ok…ok. That's a good idea," he says. "Did they give you any kind of prognosis?" he adds.

"The doctor said that it looks like they caught it soon enough that I could be cured," I say.

"That's good news," he says. We say our goodbyes and hang up. I hand the phone to Maggie.

"Well done, Sis," she says as she starts scrolling through my pictures of him. She stops and studies each for a moment, then says, "Poor guy."

I snuggle in close to her and we look at them together. After a moment, I say, "Yeah, poor guy."

Chapter 3 Captain Pennyworth

Dr. Milward's office is your typical doctor's office except for a giant pirate ship that takes up half the waiting room. Apparently, they also treat children at this office. Maggie squeals when she sees it and makes a beeline straight for the ship. Either she hasn't seen the sign stating the age and height restrictions or she has downright ignored it because within seconds she's climbing all over it. She stands at the helm and says in her most authoritative pirate voice, "Swab the decks ye bilge rats!" She thrusts her bent index finger meant to be a pirate's hook into the air for emphasis and yells, "Arrrr!" Next, she jumps down from the deck, pulls an imaginary sword from her nonexistent scabbard, and commences to fight an invisible opponent.

The children who are already playing there when she commandeers the ship stare at her in disbelief. They sidle away in alarm. Then one bald, little boy about four years old takes one look at the action and runs the length of the waiting room to join her. In seconds they're sparring with their imaginary swords, swinging in to save the day, and carrying off the booty, which just happens to be Maggie's actual boot. The entire waiting room and staff watch, enthralled with the action. The play only comes to an end when the nurse calls my name. Maggie bows to the little boy and says, "Until we meet again, my worthy young opponent."

"Aye, aye ya thcurvy, thcum!" he yells at her through the gap left by two missing front teeth. Maggie salutes him and follows me through the door toward the exam rooms.

We follow the nurse down the hall to a corner where she weighs me. I'm glad I'm fully clothed because when Maggie sees my weight, she makes a muffled gasping sound. I look at her and give her a look that I hope says, "Don't go there girlfriend." The nurse then measures my height and leads us to a room where she motions for me to sit on the exam table. As I try to daintily settle myself on the crinkling paper that covers the table, Mom and Maggie take the empty chairs along the wall. The nurse takes my vitals and asks me a lot of health questions, the whole time typing the information into the computer. When she's done, she tells us that the doctor will be right in, and she leaves. The room is suddenly silent and somber, and I can't stand it. There's a life size, plastic skeleton in the corner of the room. I decide to use it to lighten the mood. I stand behind it, and while moving the arms, I talk for it.

"Hello, my name is…" I think for a moment then say, "My name is Captain Pennyworth." I extend the skeleton's hand to Mom and Maggie. They chuckle. "How rude!" I have the captain say. "Will you not shake hands with me? Or do you have something against skinny men?" This elicits a heartier laugh from them. I poke my head around and say, "I feel like he needs one of those three cornered hats and a captain's jacket."

As I settle myself again on the crinkly paper, there's a knock on the door. I yell, "Come in." The door opens and a small, gray-haired man comes in carrying a laptop with the nurse behind him. His eyes remain glued to the screen. A stethoscope is draped around his neck and an assortment of pens fill the pocket of his green and blue plaid, button-up shirt. His loose-fitting khaki pants bag around his ankles and it looks like the brown leather belt he's wearing is the only thing holding them up. It isn't until he's standing directly in front of me that he looks up from the screen. He looks a bit startled when he sees me for the first time. He extends his hand and says, "Dr. Milward, and you must be Jennifer."

I shake his hand and nod. Then he turns and introduces himself to Mom and Maggie. Once he's done with that, he settles himself on the small, round swiveling chair, crosses his legs, nestling his laptop in his lap and studies the screen. Dr. Milward then walks to my side and puts his cold stethoscope on my chest listening to my heart and lungs. He then looks in my ears, mouth, and nose. I lie down and he pushes on my abdomen and listens to my stomach. He helps me sit up and moves back to his chair and enters information from his brief exam into the computer. After a few moments of silence, he looks up and says, "Well, it looks as if your cancer is at a stage III." He starts rattling off a bunch of medical jargon to explain how the stomach works. When he starts describing how the stomach has three layers, I feel myself getting squeamish and have to tune him out. I stare out the window instead. The trees are covered in white and pink blossoms. I watch as the breeze breaks loose some of the petals and they gently float down to the green carpet of grass. They look very much like tiny ballerinas endlessly twirling.

I'm jolted back to reality when Mom puts her hand on my knee and says, "Will that work for you, Sweetheart?"

"I'm sorry. I wasn't listening. What are we talking about?"

"The doctor wants to schedule the surgery for next week."

"Surgery? Uh…I guess so. What will you be operating on?"

"Your stomach, you ding dong!" Maggie interjects with a chuckle. Leave it to her to be the comic relief.

"We'll be removing the tumor. Then you'll start chemotherapy the following week," Dr. Milward continues.

The reality of it all sinks in, causing my chest to tighten up and I feel as if I'm going to vomit…again. I don't even realize I'm shaking until Mom puts her arm around me. "Are you cold, Sweetheart? Would you like a blanket?" she asks.

I shake my head and weakly tell Dr. Milward, "Next week will be fine."

"Ok," Dr. Milward says, just a little too chipper for my liking. "Doris, my office manager, will make those arrangements. Make sure you visit with her before you leave." With that he unceremoniously ends our appointment, he and the nurse both leave.

As Mom gathers up her things, Maggie goes to Captain Pennyworth and takes him in her arms, dancing him around the room. Mom and I laugh. Just then the nurse returns with written instructions on how to prepare for the surgery.

When she sees Maggie embracing the skeleton she says, "Now, no stealing my boyfriend." Laughing, Maggie puts Captain Pennyworth back where he belongs. As we follow the nurse out of the room Maggie bids the skeleton farewell and blows him a kiss. The nurse then leads us to Doris where we make arrangements for the surgery.

The car is silent as Mom drives. She announces she needs a few things from the grocery store, so she pulls into the parking lot. Maggie and I decide to stay in the car. Mom leaves us with the promise she won't be very long. Maggie and I sit in silence, each of us in our own thoughts. The weight of my upcoming surgery becomes too heavy for me.

"I've never had an operation before. Maggie, I'm scared," I blurt out,

She reaches up from the backseat, and putting her hand on my shoulder says, "I know. I'm scared too. But Mom and I are here for you, and we'll get through this together."

I appreciate her sentiments and nod my head acknowledging my understanding, but her commitment brings me little comfort. I'm the one who'll be under the knife. I'm the one who'll have to go through chemo. We lapse back into silence. After a few more minutes Mom comes back and we're on the road again.

As Mom turns onto our street, I try to commit it all to memory, the road as it rises for a short distance and then curves to the right before it plunges down to our section of street. I look at all the ranch style homes with their lush green lawns and tall pines. Spring flowers trim the yards, adding a border to the shrubbery. I want it to always be a part of me no matter where I am.

As we approach our house, I see someone sitting on our front step. It takes me a moment to realize who it is. I gasp, which scares Mom. She slams on the brake, reflexively putting her arm out to brace me and yells, "What? What is it?"

I point at the man on the doorstep and before I can say a word Maggie asks, "Is that Hunter?"

I just stare at him, nodding. "Uh huh."

Mom pulls into the driveway, and before she can even put the car in park Maggie is out the door. She practically runs up to him and with a grin extends her hand saying, "You must be Hunter."

With a bewildered smile Hunter takes her hand and says, "And you must be Maggie."

"He knows my name," she squeals as if she were meeting a celebrity. She twirls around and plops down beside him. He chuckles, seeming to be very captivated by her. Mom and I remain by the car, watching. I can't help feeling as if I'm seeing something very magical happening. Mom begins to step toward them, but I put out my hand to hold her back. They continue talking for a few minutes before they realize we are there.

Hunter stands up, comes to me, and embraces me. "What are you doing here?" I ask.

He shrugs his shoulders and says, "I was just so worried about you. I had to be here…to support you." He leans in and kisses my cheek.

"Awww! How sweet," Maggie says looking at Hunter like a lost puppy dog.

We hear a clap of thunder, and it begins to sprinkle. "Why don't we move this party inside?" Mom suggests. Hunter grabs his bag, and we head into the living room.

We barely sit down to visit when Hunter asks, "Are there any good hotels close by?"

"Nonsense!" Maggie declares, "You can stay with us. We have a hide-a-bed in the den." Maggie doesn't notice Mom's look of consternation as she leads Hunter down the hall to the den. I look at Mom, shrug my shoulders and follow them to Hunter's *new* room.

Chapter 4 Hunter's First Visit

I wake the next morning to the sound of Maggie's laughter lilting through the house. I follow the sound and find her sitting cross-legged on the end of the fold-out bed. Hunter's lying under the covers looking like he just woke up. His sandy blonde hair stands up in spots and he's shirtless. I watch Maggie's eyes take in the details of his chiseled physique. She's still in her pajamas, the pink, baby doll ones, the ones that show off her shapely legs.

I should be jealous, I think, but I just don't have the energy to worry about it. Besides, I like how they look together. He's looking handsome as always, even having just woken up. His eyes are twinkling, and his smile is shy. I don't remember him ever looking at me that way. I file this information away for later examination. I clear my throat to let them know I'm there. Maggie whirls around and smiles. She jumps up and grabs my hand, drawing me into the room.

"Oh, Jenn!" She exclaims. "Hunter and I were just talking about going for a hike today. I want him to see our beautiful countryside before he has to leave tomorrow. You're coming, right?" I want to scoff because I'm in no shape to go traipsing around the countryside. I'm shocked she'd even consider it, but then I remind myself that all this cancer stuff is new to them as well.

I take a deep breath and say, "I think you better go without me."

"Aww," Maggie whines, her face turning into an adorable pout. I shake my head.

"We'll help you," Hunter says, comprehending why I don't want to go.

"Thanks for the offer, Hunter, but I think you'll enjoy it more if you don't have to worry about me. Go ahead, I'll be fine." Maggie looks hesitant, but finally she reluctantly agrees.

With that decided I go to the kitchen, leaving them to plan their hike. I find Mom at the table staring at her phone smiling.

"That good, huh?" I say. She jumps and puts her phone face down on the table.

"Oh, you scared me," she says, an odd smile on her face. I look at her suspiciously.

"Sorry I scared you."

"What?" she asks when I stare at her a bit too long.

"What's with that goofy grin?" I ask.

"Goofy grin?" she asks just as her text tone chimes. She tries to nonchalantly ignore it, but I can tell she's itching to read it. She gets up and walks toward the sink but suddenly changes directions and opens the cupboard to retrieve dishes. She takes them to the table and begins setting the table even though nothing is cooking. She picks up her phone to make room for a plate, an obvious ruse.

"Mom, who are you texting?" I finally ask, incredibly curious.

"Nunya," she says with a little giggle.

"Nunya? Who's Nunya?" I ask.

"Nunya business," she says with a sassy tilt of her head. I stare at her, stunned by her juvenile behavior.

Just then, Maggie enters the kitchen and asks, "What's going on?"

I turn and say, "Mom's been texting someone and won't tell me who."

"So, what's the big deal about that?" Maggie says.

"Because she giggles like a teenage girl talking to a boy when she reads the texts. I think it's a man."

"Reeeally?" Maggie says, suddenly interested. "I wonder who it could be. Shall we guess?" she says with a mischievous smile.

"Yes, I think we must," I say. We begin naming every available man we can think of from the postman to Maggie's math teacher from her senior year in high school, waiting for the reaction that will give Mom away, but we're disappointed.

When we've exhausted our list of men, Maggie and I look at each other.

"What about that hunky doctor you were telling me about? The one Mom was flirting with while you were recovering from your endoscopy," Maggie says.

"I was *not* flirting with him," she insists indignantly, her face turning bright red. *BINGO!* Just the reaction we were looking for.

"It *IS* him!" I yell. Maggie and I laugh hysterically.

"Oh stop, you two!" she demands in a futile attempt to do damage control.

"Oh, Mom, I'm happy for you," I say.

"Yeah, Mom, it's about time," Maggie says, and we both move in for hugs.

"Really?" Mom asks, "You don't mind? I mean we've just been texting. He hasn't asked me out yet, and it could all come to nothing."

"Really, Mom," Maggie begins, "we want you to be happy. Now read us those texts."

Mom giggles and says, "You really want to hear them?"

"Of course!" we say in unison.

We move to the table where she reads us the texts. I hear Hunter get into the shower while Maggie and I live vicariously through our mother's texts.

What a turnaround, I think, *the daughters living through the mother's experiences.*

I smell his aftershave before Hunter walks in. He stands awkwardly in the doorway having heard the last bit of the text Mom was reading to us.

"Am I interrupting something?" he asks. I take him in, once again awed by his chiseled features and muscular body. His wavy, blonde hair is slicked back in a way that is reminiscent of the '50's bad boys. I hear a sharp intake of air from my right. I turn and see Maggie engrossed in her veneration of Hunter.

"Come on in," Mom says, getting up from the table. "I'll get some breakfast going."

Maggie waves him over and says, patting the chair next to her, "Come sit here."

"Let me help you, Mom," I say getting up from the table. I feel guilty leaving her to do all the cooking.

"Thanks, Honey," she says and hands me the eggs she'd just retrieved from the fridge. Maggie and Hunter sit together at the table chatting, oblivious to Mom and me.

"I've never seen this side of Hunter before," I whisper to Mom.

Mom looks over at the two of them and says thoughtfully, "Really? How do you feel about your sister's adoration of your boyfriend?"

I shrug my shoulders and say, "I'm not sure. I'm definitely not jealous. Actually, I think they look good together."

Mom considers them thoughtfully and says, "Indeed they do."

After breakfast, Maggie gets dressed, and she and Hunter get ready for their hike. Mom fixes them a lunch and I make myself comfortable on the couch determined to watch a movie. I go through hundreds of channels only to settle on reruns of "Gilligan's Island." I try to get involved in the story, but I'm distracted by Maggie as she scurries around collecting every possible thing they could ever need.

"Honestly, Maggie," Mom says, "you're going to be gone for only a couple of hours."

"I know," Maggie says nonchalantly, "but it's better to be prepared."

"But," Mom replies, "it'll be too heavy to carry."

"I'll carry the pack," Hunter interjects. "I went camping with some friends of mine last summer and if I hadn't taken all the things I took, my buddy Sam would have died."

"Really?" Mom says surprised.

At the exact same moment, Maggie says, "See?" Hunter looks back and forth from one to the other not knowing which conversation to continue.

Finally, he nods at Maggie then turns to Mom and says, "Yes, as a Boy Scout I was taught to always be prepared, so in my pack I had a complete Med kit, among some other things like pen and paper, which proved to be a lifesaver. During that campout my buddies and I went hiking. About mid-way through our hike Sam decided to chew gum. I told him not to because he might choke on it. Well, of course he didn't listen and when he tripped over a log a little later, he inhaled his gum. Mike tried the Heimlich maneuver, but the gum was so wedged in there we couldn't get it out. Tim ran to get help, but I knew Sam would die if we didn't act fast. As luck would have it, just the night before I'd watched a video on how to perform an emergency tracheotomy, so I pulled the scalpel out of my Med kit and slit open his throat right here," he said pointing to the hollow at the base of his throat. "Then I unscrewed the bottom half of the pen and carefully inserted it into his trachea. Man, I was sweating bullets because he didn't start breathing right away, so I put my mouth over the pen in his neck and blew. His chest rose so I knew the tracheotomy had worked. It only took one blow to get him to start breathing again on his own. When the paramedics arrived, they said if it hadn't been for my tracheotomy, he would have died."

Maggie grabs Hunter's bulging bicep and, nearly swooning, says, "I feel so safe around you." I turn to Mom whose saucer-sized eyeballs protrude from her now pale face. For a moment I think she might swoon as well, but not because she's impressed. She plops onto the couch at my feet, causing me to snort with laughter.

"I'll go get a pen just in case you need to perform an emergency tracheotomy," Maggie says as she runs to the kitchen in search of a pen suitable for the procedure. As they leave, Mom stares after them still wide-eyed.

Once the door closes behind them, she turns to me and asks, "Is he for real?"

I chuckle and say, "I actually know Sam, and yes, every bit of it is true."

I didn't think Mom's eyes could get any bigger, but they do as she exclaims, "Seriously?"

At this, I laugh heartily. Mom joins me, and we laugh until our sides hurt.

As the laughter subsides, she wraps her arms around me, silently holding me as if she fears letting me go would destroy her. I fall asleep in her arms and slip into a dream.

I'm on the outcrop of rock again. The ocean breeze refreshes my skin and makes me feel alive. I close my eyes and embrace the feeling. A hand brushes mine and I open my eyes. Jack is standing at my side. He too is staring out to sea. His hair has been cut, his beard trimmed and is wearing clean clothes.

"Hello, stranger," I say, "It's been a while since we've met like this."

He nods then says, "But I've been by your side the whole time."

"That's a little creepy," I say with a cheeky smile.

At first, he looks confused and a little worried, but then he notices my smile and simply says, "It was only meant to be supportive." I elbow him playfully and scamper down the rock and start walking along the beach. He chuckles, it's deep and hearty, and quickly follows me. In no time he falls into step with me. The tide is on its way out leaving behind in its wake all sorts of life. The moist sand squelches beneath our feet. Bubbles begin to form in it as creatures start to realize their haven has disappeared. I nearly step on a baby turtle as it extracts itself from its dissolving shelter. I quickly sidestep it and watch as it scurries toward the protection of the ocean. Jack waits for me and we're soon walking side-by-side again.

"So, sailor, tell me about yourself," I say. "You seem to know a lot about me, so I figure you owe me a life story."

"Where should I start?" he asks, fidgeting nervously.

"You could start by telling me where you were born."

"Okay, I was born in a small mill town in the east," he says.

"Which state?"

"Massachusetts."

"Your town had a mill?"

He nods.

"What did they mill there?"

"Charcoal for gunpowder."

"Gunpowder? I've never given a single thought to how gunpowder is made."

"In our town, there was also a factory, which turned the charcoal into gunpowder. Our town provided a vast amount of gunpowder to the army during the war."

"Which war?"

"The Spanish American War."

"Huh!" was all I said. I really don't know how to respond to that. So, I change the subject and ask, "So, what did you do for entertainment?"

"There wasn't a lot of leisure time with all the work needing to be done, but when there was time, my friends, my brother, and I would go to the river and swim. That's when I learned to love the water."

"You have a brother?"

"Yes, his name is Henry. He's two years older than me. I also have two older sisters as well, Abigail and Mabel. They both married young and moved to Boston. Between the two of them, they have a passel of kids."

"What about Henry? Where is he?"

His face suddenly takes on a haunted look. *What could have happened to Henry to cause Jack to look that way?* I wonder.

Jack coughs and tentatively begins, "When Henry was sixteen, he started working at the factory. He'd been working there for almost a year when there was an explosion. It killed twenty-three men. Henry was severely burned. They brought him to our home. We cared for him the best we could…but he only lived two more days."

"That must have been horrible."

"When I saw the agony he was in, I could hardly stand it. My prayers changed from asking God to spare his life to asking God to end his misery." He looked at the ground. "The next day, he was gone."

"I'm so sorry. That must have been extremely hard," I say, putting my hand on his arm. He smiles sadly and puts his hand on mine.

"Thank you for your compassion."

I thread my arm through his and we walk amiably down the beach, each lost in our own thoughts. "When did you become a sailor?" I ask.

"After Henry died, my parents weren't the same. They became angry, and since I was the only one left at home…well, I was a convenient target. When I turned fifteen, I decided I'd had enough and left. I went as far as New York where I worked several different jobs. None of them for very long. A friend decided to join the Navy and convinced me to also join. I figured it was a good fit since I loved the ocean and because the steady work would mean I wouldn't have to go hungry anymore."

"Did you like it?"

"At first. Each port was such an adventure. But once the novelty of traveling to new countries wore off, I found I was lonely."

"Lonely? On a ship full of people and you felt lonely? Wasn't there anyone you could be friends with?"

"There were a few people, but the friendly ones never lasted more than a couple of years. They would leave for new adventures or to settle down and start a family. It seemed like only the cranky ones stayed, or maybe they became cranky because they stayed. And when you see the same crotchety men day after day, you learn to avoid them. It was easier that way. Besides, I wanted to get married and start a family of my own."

"So, did you?"

"Did I what?"

"Get married and have a family?"

He shakes his head and says, "I'm tired of talking about me. It's my turn to ask you questions."

"Fair enough."

"Where were you born?" he asks.

"I thought you knew everything about me. We're old friends, right?"

"Can anyone know everything about someone?"

"Yeah, but my birth is so basic. Most people who're friends know those kinds of things about each other."

Jack sighs, gives me a withering look, and says, "Just answer my questions...*please.*"

I huff and say, "Fine. I was born in Portland, Oregon. I've lived there my whole life except for the last three years when I've been studying at the University of Oregon. Go Ducks! I was studying English...well, until my life got derailed by cancer." I thrust my fist into the air and say sarcastically, "Yay me!"

Jack chuckles and says, "You know, there are worse things than dying."

"Oh really?" I say, my voice dripping with sarcasm, "and what might those be?"

"Living an unfulfilled life or one full of hate."

"Like mine if I die?"

"I know people who lived just a short time who were able to fill their lives full of meaning. You can do that, too."

"Really? How am I supposed to do that if I'm too sick to even get out of bed?"

"I'll help you. We can start right now. In the town, there's a concert. We could attend that."

"What town?"

"The one just up that hill," he says pointing to a small hill several yards away. I look and see some treetops and roof lines just beyond it.

"I've never noticed that before. Weird."

"Come with me," he says, grabbing my hand and pulling me toward the town. As we approach the hill, I see earthen steps roughly cut into the hillside. With each step up, more of the town becomes visible. First there's a park with tall trees rising up from a carpet of grass. Wooden benches encircle a small playground where there are swings, a slide, a teeter totter, and a small, wooden merry-go-round. The park is flanked on three sides by houses and on the fourth side is an unpaved road where the steps come to an end.

I look around and see that the road extends several blocks in both directions. To the right there are just more houses. They're small wooden ones with tiny, well-trimmed lawns. To the left there are businesses: a market, a hardware store, a barber shop, and a saloon. We go left, walking past the barber shop with its red and white striped pole. We hear the barber chatting with his customers before we reach the open doorway. There's a man sitting in the barber's chair arguing with the customers who are waiting their turn. His handlebar mustache twitches as he talks. I hear the clomping of horses' hooves as carriages pass by.

When we come to a corner, we turn left and walk two more blocks until we arrive in front of a concert hall. Other people are arriving at the same time we do. The women are wearing fine dresses with hats and parasols. Worried I'm horribly underdressed, I look down at my clothes. To my surprise, I'm no longer wearing my skirt and blouse but a pale blue gown as beautiful as the others. My hair is piled up on my head with a delicate hat perched on top of my curls. Amazed, I look at Jack and realize he's no longer wearing his sailor's uniform, but a fine black wool suit, waistcoat, and white starched collar tied with a black necktie. I must admit he looks very dashing. He smiles at me, causing my heart to quiver.

Feeling confident, we walk into the concert hall. The wooden floor creaks as we walk across it. The hall isn't fancy, but it's large with a small stage on the opposite end of the room. To the right is a door marked kitchen with a pass-through counter next to it. Its doors are thrown open and there are cakes, pies, and cookies ready to be cut and served. Next to them are stacks of plates, silverware, and cups for coffee. Mismatched chairs are arranged in rows in the center of the floor. We slide past a couple seated on the end of the row and go to the middle of the row. Before I have a chance to sit down Jack moves behind my chair and holds it for me. I reach around my skirt to smooth it down before I sit, how Mom taught me, and discover I have a bustle I go to sit down but then realize I don't know how to sit in a chair wearing a bustle. I make a couple of futile attempts then look at Jack embarrassed I lean in close and quietly ask, "How am I supposed to sit down with this bustle?"

He smiles and replies, "Just lift it a bit as you sit. Oh, and just perch on the chair. Don't slide all the way back."

"That sounds really uncomfortable," I hiss.

"You'll be fine. Trust me," he says looking quite amused by the whole situation. I do as he says and to my surprise, I discover that my bustle is made of collapsible wire. I have no problem sitting down but still worry I won't be comfortable perching for who knows how long. As I get situated, I realize I'm also wearing a corset.

I wiggle around testing its feel and think, *Wow, these things are a lot more comfortable than I thought they'd be.*

Once settled I look around at the other audience members as they take their seats. I see someone who looks like our mail carrier but with a handlebar mustache waxed to a point. With him is a woman who reminds me of my third-grade teacher, Ms. Pendleton. Several other people from the audience remind me of people from my life. I realize that's how dreams work, filling in the void with images already in your memory.

The performers walk onto the stage carrying stringed instruments and take their places. A man steps onto the stage and addresses the audience.

"Welcome, ladies and gentlemen! Thank you for joining us for this presentation of Vivaldi's *The Four Seasons*. We'd like to thank the Portland Orchestra for coming all this way to our little town to share this wonderful music with us. Ladies and gentlemen, let's give them a round of applause." As he steps down from the stage and takes his seat, one of the violinists plays a note, and the other twenty or so musicians tune their instruments to that note, creating quite a cacophony. A few moments later, they all quiet down, and the conductor enters the stage. The audience erupts into applause. The conductor bows, steps onto the podium, turns to the orchestra, and signals with his baton for them to start playing.

I lean over to Jack and whisper, "I've never been to a live performance."

"Well then, you're in for a treat," he whispers.

The music starts out with *Spring*, a sprightful tune eliciting images of lambs prancing around a pasture and birds chirping in the trees. I sit in awe as I watch the skillfulness of the performers. It almost makes me want to learn to play the violin. The music sounds like birds chirping. Before I know it, the music has moved onto *Summer*. It alternates between placid, melodic tunes and rapid, exciting music. The program indicates that it represents sudden summer thunderstorms. As *Autumn* begins, I hear the festivals and frivolity of the peasants as they dance and drink in the cool autumn air. Suddenly the music softens and makes me feel sleepy.

Maybe the peasants have fallen asleep and are dreaming? I think. The next part of *Autumn* is supposed to be a hunt, but it makes me think of rich snobby people dancing very primly.

Winter starts and it's supposed to sound like snowflakes falling and teeth chattering. I guess I can hear that. Really it just makes me want to dance, and I find my foot tapping. The next movement is called *Rain*. The rhythm does sound like rain falling. The final movement starts out so peaceful and sweet, conjuring thoughts of a professional ice skater performing a beautiful routine. Then two melodies intertwine with one another going up and down the scales and finally merging into one. The music crescendos, coming to a crashing climax then spirals down to a sweet, final cord. Something happens to me in that moment as the audience applauds. I feel something I've never felt before. It's as if the music has unlocked joy inside me. Sparks of it swell in me, and I feel as if I've been filled with beauty. It shoots to my extremities, filling me with warmth and enchantment. After a few moments, I realize Jack is watching me. I turn and see him smiling. A blush creeps up my neck and across my cheeks. Embarrassed, I look down at the program I'm holding. I fiddle with it for a few minutes then realize I can use it to cool my blush.

I'm still fanning myself when I realize that the audience is giving the orchestra a standing ovation. I lay the program on the floor, rise to my feet and clap enthusiastically. Someone close by whistles. I look to see who it was and realize that it had been Jack. I laugh.

The musicians bow and exit the stage while the audience abandons their seats and begins mingling. A few moments later, the musicians reappear through a side door and join the crowd. They eventually wander over to the open kitchen to get some refreshments. Amidst the clatter of dishes and all the chatter, I can't help but see Jack through new eyes. I feel so grateful that he brought me to this concert so I could experience the performance. I smile as I look at him, feeling something new and warm for him.

"Would you like some refreshment?" he asks. I smile and nod. While he's gone, I look around the room and watch the people as they socialize.

I hear a mother chastising her young son for taking another piece of pie. He quickly wolfs it down and runs away. I chuckle as he whizzes past me. Jack returns with a piece of lemon meringue pie on a large glass plate for each of us. Next to the pie is a saucer of fruit punch and a fork. The cup is nestled in a divot in the plate. There's a raised ring around the divot that perfectly matches the size of the cup. I admire how the plate is cleverly designed to have a stable place for the cup.

"Thank you," I say and take the plate from him.

Just then I hear the same mother who had chastised her son a few moments before screech, "Stinky! Stinky Flatasheck! You get back here right now!" Bewildered, I turn in time to see the same young boy darting through the crowd with a handful of cake. Crumbs fly as he weaves his way between suits and gowns.

I look at Jack and ask, "Stinky is his name?"

He shrugs his shoulders and says, "Some people don't have much of an imagination when it comes to names."

"Or maybe too much," I interject. Just then the boy dashes out the door slamming it behind him. Jack and I look at each other and laugh.

When I'm finished with my refreshments, Jack takes my plate, adds it to his, and returns them to the kitchen. He comes back quickly, offers me his arm, and we walk out into the sunlight.

Silently we walk, then I turn and say, "Thank you for bringing me to the concert. I really enjoyed it."

He looks at me from the corner of his eye, smiling, and says, "You are very welcome. I'm glad you liked it."

We stroll down the street, looking through the windows at the goods being sold. For me it's like walking through a museum, but here the goods are shiny and new. I can't help wondering what things from my day my grandchildren will find in a museum...a smartphone, a tablet, a laptop?

"Would you like some ice cream?" Jack asks. My mind is jerked from my imagination, and I stare at him wide-eyed.

"Ice cream?"

"Yes. You have heard of it, haven't you?"

"Yes, yes I have. It's just, how…I mean, you have ice cream in this time period?"

He looks at me and chuckles, "Yes, we have ice cream. In fact, some form of ice cream has been around since before the birth of Christ. Did you know that George Washington once spent over $200 dollars for ice cream throughout the summer of 1790?"

"That's a lot of money even by my standards," I say. "Why did he do that?"

"It's said he really liked ice cream and when he became president, he made sure there were plenty of ice cream spoons and dishes, so he'd never have to be without his favorite dessert."

Jack offers me his hand and says in an unusually formal voice, "Let us partake of this delight then."

I smile at his sudden divergence into silliness, put my hand in his, stick my nose in the air, and imitate his formal voice, saying, "Yes, let's." We strut down the street like a pair of pretentious peacocks. Once we arrive outside the shop, we drop our pompous air. Jack pushes open the door, causing a small bell attached to the door to tinkle. The shop is small. A bar stretches along the side wall. Round stools run parallel to the bar, and on the other side there are large cabinets which hold everything ice cream. In a glass case near the door are six containers of ice cream. I read the signs. There's chocolate, vanilla, peach, strawberry, huckleberry, and citron. *What the heck is citron?* I wonder.

A young man, not much older than sixteen, steps forward dressed like he's part of a barbershop quartet. He smiles a very toothy grin and asks, "What would you folks like?" Jack turns to me and asks, "Which flavor would you like?"

I tap my chin as I look over the options. "May I taste the citron? I'm really curious as to how it tastes."

"Why, yes, ma'am," the clerk says, taking a small wooden spoon, scooping up a sample and handing it to me. "You'll find it to have a citrus taste, ma'am. Somewhat like lemon except it has less of a sharp taste."

I put the spoon in my mouth and taste the confection. "Mmmmm," is all I can say. "I'll definitely have some of that."

"Dish me up a scoop as well," Jack says to the grinning clerk and hands him some coins.

"Have a seat, and I'll bring it right out to you," the young man says.

We walk to the nearest table. I perch delicately on the edge of the seat like Jack instructed me earlier, being careful not to smash my bustle. Within a few minutes, the young clerk brings our ice cream, and we indulge.

"I wish I could get a picture of myself in this dress," I say nonchalantly. "Maggie would laugh herself silly seeing me in it."

Jack's eyes light up and he declares, "We can. A photo studio just opened down the street. We can go there when we're done with our ice cream."

I smile, not thinking about how I would ever get a photograph from my dreams to Maggie to see – I just don't want my time with Jack to end yet.

Once our ice cream is gone Jack leads me to the photo studio. I look at him and ask, "Do I have any ice cream on my face? I don't want my picture taken with a dirty face."

"No. You look beautiful," he says, and that annoying blush returns. No one has ever described me as beautiful before. "Do I have any on my face?" He asks, shooting me a cheesy grin. I inspect his face and notice a smudge of ice cream on his chin.

"Um…actually there's some ice cream on your chin right there," I say pointing to my own chin to demonstrate where to find the smudge.

"Really?" he says and sticks his tongue out as far as he can trying to lick away the troublesome ice cream. I can't help but giggle at how silly he looks.

Finally, I take pity on him and apply some of my own spit to my thumb and wipe his chin clean. He looks at me intensely, takes my hand in his, and gently kisses my palm. A gasp escapes me, and intense emotions threaten to overpower me. I pull my hand away and look at the window display. I hear him clear his throat. Then he asks, "Are you ready?"

I turn to him, my heart still pounding, and nod. We walk into the shop, and just as we do there's a simultaneous *click, poof,* and flash of light, which causes me to jump.

"Very good," a man says as he extracts himself from under a black drape that's attached to a wooden, boxy camera on a tripod. A smile spreads across my face. The man who had been sitting for his picture stands up. Behind him is a strange framework attached to the chair he'd been sitting in.

"What is that?" I ask, pointing to the framework.

"What?" Jack says.

"What are those long metal poles attached to the chair for?"

"Oh, they're to keep one's body immobilized during the long exposure time," he explains. I nod my head and try to imagine what it would be like to sit in it.

We wait while the customer writes his address on a form and pays the photographer.

"Now then," the photographer says. "Check back at the beginning of next week. Your photo should be ready by then."

The man tips his hat and says, "Thank you very much."

The photographer bows his head in the direction of the man and says, "And thank you for your business." He holds the door for the man. Once he's gone and the door is closed, he turns to us and says, "And what can I do for you?"

"We would like our photo taken," Jack says.

"Very good. Come right over here," the photographer says as he ushers us over to the chair. He motions for me to sit down. When I do, he adjusts the framework to fit my stature. Then from a cabinet he retrieves another framework for someone who's standing and puts it just behind the left corner of the chair. He motions for Jack to stand in front of it. Jack obeys and the framework is adjusted to him. The photographer then fiddles with the camera, replacing plates or something. It reminds me of how the technician readied the x-ray machine before taking my x-ray a few days ago. In a few moments, he's ready. "All right then," he says, then ducks under the black cloth draped around the back of the camera. I smile and try to look pretty for the picture. "No! No, no you don't smile," he says.

I'm a bit shocked but then remember that during this era they didn't smile for pictures. "Oh, I'm so sorry," I say and try to look as serious as I possibly can. Unfortunately, I can't. A giggle bubbles up from inside me and threatens to burst out.

Don't smile, I command myself but just as he snaps the picture a closed mouth smile creeps across my face.

"Stay perfectly still," he demands. I freeze, hold my breath, and hope I don't look like an idiot. After a few moments, he covers the lens and allows us to move. I sigh with relief as a drop of sweat rolls down my face. I get up and we move to the counter where Jack pays the photographer, and he writes us a receipt.

"Check back in a week and I'll have your photo ready for you," the photographer says.

"Next week?" I almost blurt then remind myself, this isn't 2022 where pictures are instantaneous.

We walk outside just as an old car passes by—well, old for my time period but very new for Jack's. The driver squeezes the bulb of the horn. I expect an "awooga" sound to come out but instead I hear snoring. Puzzled, I look at Jack just as he and the world around me fades to black. I hear snoring again and open my eyes. My head is now in Mom's lap, and she's fallen asleep as well. Her head is flopped onto the back of the couch, with her mouth wide open, and she is emitting a loud snore. All of a sudden, her head pops up and she groggily asks, "Who was making that noise?"

I laugh and say, "Mom, it was you. You were snoring."

"Was I?" I nod. She wipes her mouth and says, "Well, that was attractive."

Just then we hear the jangle of Maggie's keys in the door. She and Hunter come into the house looking like the cat who just ate the canary. "How was the hike?" Mom asks.

Maggie smiles, "It was great."

"Hunter?"

He jumps when he hears his name.

"Did you enjoy yourself?" Mom asks.

He glances at Maggie, smiles, and replies, "I had a wonderful time." Then turns to Mom and adds, "The countryside is beautiful." Again, he looks at Maggie, his eyes lingering a bit too long. It's a good thing I'm not the jealous type.

Chapter 5 Surgery

The day of the surgery comes all too fast. Thankfully I am the surgeon's first "customer" so I don't have to sit around for hours worrying, and neither does Mom.

"Let's get this over with," I say when they call me back. We approach a set of double doors. The nurse walks to a small, black, square panel on the wall and taps her ID badge on it, causing the doors to hiss open. Mom and I follow her through and down a hallway. She directs us to a small alcove-ish room similar to the one at the Digestive Health Center.

A man is standing at the computer typing in information. Once I'm seated on the gurney, he turns, extends his hand, and introduces himself, "Hi, I'm Nate and I'm your nurse today."

I'm not sure how I feel about having a man be my nurse. It feels a little awkward, but he seems as friendly and capable as any female nurse. So why not?

He instructs me to change into a gown and pulls the curtain across the doorway as he steps out. I quickly change into the gown and settle onto the gurney. It's cold in the room or at least it feels cold to me, so I pull the blanket up over me. A few minutes later, he comes back and puts an identification bracelet on my wrist, quizzes me on my name, birthday, etc. It feels like a repeat of the endoscopy.

I start to shiver. I'm not sure if it's from fear or from the cold or both. I try not to let it show but he notices and brings me a blanket that's been in a warmer. The delicious warmth seeps down to my bones and stops my shivering.

Once I'm all prepped with registration, an IV, and a gown, the surgeon, Dr. Jolly, comes in to introduce herself and go over the possible risks. I guess legally she has to, but all it does is make me want to get up and leave. If I hadn't been attached to the bed by the IV, I might have.

When she finishes terrifying me, Mom says to the doctor, "I went to school with a Chris Jolly. By chance, are you related to him?"

Dr. Jolly smiles and says, "Yes, he's my youngest brother."

"Really? I haven't seen him in years. How's he doing?" Leave it to Mom to find a connection with my surgeon. No matter where we go, she knows someone or finds a person connected to someone she knows. I tune them out and let them have their reminiscing conversation.

Instead, I think about Jack. I picture how his dark loose curls spill out from under his hat, how his eyes sparkle when he smiles. The nurse comes back and interrupts my musing to inject something into my IV tube. I feel my body relax and the world fades to black...and then I'm with Jack. We're sitting silently on the beach staring out to sea, listening to the crash of the waves and the cawing of the seagulls. He's close enough that I can smell him. He smells of salt and leather. Strangely enough, I like it. It's comforting.

"What would you like to do today?" he asks. I shrug my shoulders. "The carnival's in town," he eagerly says. "We could go to it. I've heard they have a Fairy Floss machine. I would love to treat you to some."

"Fairy Floss? What's that?"

"It's a special, light, flossy sweet," he says, his eyes gleaming. He looks so much like an excited little boy that I can't say no.

I chuckle and say, "Alright then, let's go. I'd love to try some of this Fairy Floss. It sounds fascinating." He stands and helps me to my feet, offering me his arm. I curtsy, say, "Thank you," and thread my arm through his. Arm in arm, we make our way up the beach to the steps leading to the town. Each step brings us closer to the town and with each step more of my senses register what's going on in the town. At first, I hear faint laughter and music. Then the smell of popcorn wafts down to us. I can also detect the rank smell of animals and new hay. Just as we're about to crest the hill, we hear an elephant trumpet. I gasp. My excitement was palpable, I say, "That was an elephant! I've never seen an elephant up close." Suddenly, *I* was the child excited about the upcoming adventure.

When we reach the top of the steps, the entire carnival comes into view. A group of high-spirited children run past us, their laughter tickling my ears. I want to follow suit, but I know I shouldn't, so I walk calmly alongside Jack. From a distance, I can see the elephant in a paddock next to an enormous red tent. The elephant is swaying back and forth, agitated by the children who are yelling and throwing rocks and dirt clods at it. The ringmaster angrily emerges from the tent and yells at the children, shooing them away. A mother grabs the hand of her crying son and drags him away from the paddock, scolding him the whole while.

We walk toward an open canopy where a large vat rattles as it spins. A man stands by it, twirling a paper cone upside down in the vat while simultaneously running the cone around the inside of it, catching tufts of colorful spun sugar on it. As he moves the cone around the vat, the spun sugar attracts more and more of its kind causing the blob on the cone to grow exponentially. A line of about twenty children anxiously waits for their turn to get their own cone of delight. As each child's turn arrives, they eagerly pay their five cents to the man and in return he hands them the cone laden with pink, delicious, spun sugar candy. I can't help myself and laugh as I recognize what Fairy Floss is. "Cotton candy!" I say.

"You've had this before?" Jack asks.

"Oh yes. When I was a teenager, my neighbor had a machine that he would rent out to school carnivals. Each year he had a booth at the county fair. I worked for him during that week. The kids would line up as long as this line just to get a taste. It looks like some things never change." We wait in line, watching the kids chatter and play as they wait for their turn to pay their nickel, and enthusiastically receive their cotton candy. I watch them taste the magical, sugary floss, as it melts on their tongues, and their hands and faces become a sticky mess. Their looks of delight at discovering this new delicacy are worth the wait. With each first taste their eyes widen; they look at the floss as if nothing could taste better, then dive voraciously into their treat, devouring it in moments. Then with hopeful eyes and sticky faces they return to their parents to beg for another nickel.

Soon it's our turn and as I carefully bite into mine, I watch Jack as he takes his first taste. At first his expression is puzzled then his lips turn upward into a smile. He smacks his lips with great satisfaction and says, "Mmmm!"

I giggle and say, "By the look on your face, I'm guessing you like Fairy Floss".

"Very much!" he says, placing a pinch of the fluffy confection on his tongue. "It melts in your mouth." I laugh and we stroll around the park while we eat. When he arrives at the last bite, he licks every minuscule particle from the paper cone then moves to his fingers. Once he's done with his fingers, he looks back longingly at the Fairy Floss machine. He feels around in his pocket for another coin but all he has is a few tickets for games and rides.

"Come on," I say and pull him toward the Ferris wheel. We wait in line with several groups of noisy teenagers, a young couple holding hands and making googly eyes at each other, and several fathers with young children pulling impatiently at their hands. I look up at the Ferris wheel and begin to reconsider my desire to ride it. It's made of wood that creaks and shudders as it goes around. As I watch it, I take a deep breath and remind myself that this is just a dream and that I really can't get hurt.

Jack turns to me and asks, "You're not scared, are you?"

I chuckle and look at him, "A little. After all, it is kind of rickety."

He looks up at the contraption but before he can say a word the ride operator ushers us into a seat. Jack eagerly climbs aboard. I tentatively sit next to him. The operator cinches a leather belt across our laps and secures a wooden bar in front of us. This makes me feel a little safer. Once again, I remind myself it's just a dream and no real harm will come to me.

If it breaks, I'll probably wake up before I hit the ground, I think. When the wheel starts to move, I squeal and grab the bar. We're lifted up into the air. I look to my left where I can see the entirety of the town and to my right the great expanse of the ocean. As the wheel dips down toward the ground again I catch a glimpse of Jack's ship bobbing up and down on the white capped waves as they rush to shore. The sight thrills me and scares me at the same time. Without thinking I grab his hand and squeeze it. He looks at me startled, but then a pleased grin spreads across his face. I realize what has happened and feel that stupid blush creeping up my face again. I quickly withdraw my hand. "I...I'm sorry," I stammer.

Jack's smile spreads clear up to his eyes making the corners crinkle in an adorable way. "It's alright. I don't mind you holding my hand," he says.

He then gently takes my hand and stroking my palm saying, "Your hands are so soft."

Dang! I think, *Why does he have to be so incredibly adorable?* I suddenly feel light-headed. I'm not sure if it's from the movement of the ride or from his touch. I suspect it's the latter. I feel an overwhelming desire to kiss him and find myself leaning toward him. Then I stop midway, taking in a deep breath of ocean air to clear my head, lean back into the seat and fold my hands in my lap.

Get a hold of yourself! I think. The rest of the ride passes in silence as I take in the sights around me. I try to concentrate on my surroundings, but all I can do is remember his touch, how he gently stroked my hand. I don't dare look at him for fear of giving into my passions.

The ride comes to an end, and we disembark. Jack takes my hand again, this time though to steady me while I step down from the platform. I don't really need his help but something about it makes me feel special, like I'm precious to him. A soft smile erupts, unbidden, from my lips. He notices and smiles as well.

We walk to a booth and buy sandwiches and lemonade. When we reach the tables set out for people to eat at, he pulls my chair out for me and I sit.

He's such a gentleman, I think. I have dated guys before who made a show of courtesy, but it was nothing more than to impress me. Once we had been dating for a while, the courtesy always faded away. But with Jack, it seems to come from his very core. After we eat, we stroll through the park, walking in amiable silence. The sun is setting now, and as we watch the peach and blue of the sky turn to reds and deep blue, I realize I've spent the whole day with Jack. A panic sweeps over me as I realize I've not spent this much time in a dream with him before. I rack my brain for details of what was happening to me before I fell asleep. Then I remember I was having surgery when this dream began.

Are they still working on me? Should I be awake by now? I wonder and shiver, looking around me for anything that will give me a clue as to what I should do. Suddenly, I feel Jack slide his jacket around my shoulders. I'm afraid the navy-blue wool, not a fabric I'm used to wearing, will be scratchy, but as I slip my arms into the sleeves, I feel the silky lining.

"Thank you," I say as I pull the jacket tight around me. I bite my nails worrying.

After a few minutes of stewing over what to do and not coming up with any answers, I turn to Jack and confess my fears. "Jack," I hesitantly begin, "We've never spent this much time together and...well...it's becoming night and I haven't woken up yet." He takes my hand and guides me to a bench overlooking the ocean; we sit, and I continue. "They were operating on me when I started dreaming and well," I pause and raise my hands to run my fingers through my hair but stop, remembering I'm wearing a hat over my updo. I sigh, putting my hands back into my lap and continue, "I don't know when I'll wake up and if I don't right away, I don't know what to do."

For a moment he silently thinks, then he takes my hand, looks me in the eyes and says, "I promise you, I will *never* leave you. We'll figure this out together." His promise pierces my soul and I gasp.

I nod my head, too afraid to speak for fear of giving into tears. Crying in front of others is a direct route to embarrassment for me. I turn away from him, pull in my top lip, stick out my bottom lip and blow into my eyes to dry them. Once I feel I've got my emotions under control, I turn back to him.

He's looking at me in a funny way and with a chuckle he asks, "What was all that about?"

A little confused, I ask, "What was what about?"

He looks at me perplexed and says, "I'm suddenly very confused."

"Me too," I say, beginning to comprehend that he probably wanted to know what I was doing when I was blowing in my eyes. Not wanting him to know I was about to cry I perpetuate the confusion. Too confused to continue the conversation, and to my great relief, he shakes his head, and we sit back quietly watching the sun as it slips past the horizon. The world gently turns into a velvety darkness.

Once the sky is too dark to see anything on the horizon, we turn our attention to our surroundings and realize we're the only ones left in the park. The townspeople and their families are now sheltering in their homes, the carnival workers have retired to their wagons. The only living things still in the park are the animals who restlessly pace their encagements and call out to the world. We hadn't even noticed the lamp lighters as they made their way around the park and down the street. I realize we're still holding hands, but I feel no desire to withdraw. In fact, I enjoy the way his thumb caresses the back of my hand.

I look at him. His attention is on the dog across the street. He must feel my stare because he turns to me and smiles. "Thank you for staying with me," I say.

"There's no other place I want to be," he says, his smile spreading to his eyes once more creating those cute wrinkles.

Drat! I think, *There's that urge to kiss him again. Get a hold of yourself, Jenn!* I become aware of music playing. At first, it's barely noticeable, but then it grows louder and more annoying. Then, I recognize Maggie's favorite song. "Do you hear that?" I ask Jack.

He shakes his head and asks, "What does it sound like?"

"Like my sister's favorite song," I say.

He smiles sadly and says, "I think that's your cue to wake up." I nod realizing he's right but...I don't want to go. As I think this, my world fades to black. I feel heavy and have to convince myself to open my eyes. I take a deep breath and in doing so feel the earbuds in my ears.

What the heck! I think. I crack my eyes open and see Maggie staring down at me smiling.

"I knew my music would do the trick. Mom was worried because you hadn't woken up yet, but I knew my tunes would bring you back to the living," she crows.

My arms feel like lead, and it takes all my strength to reach up to pull the earbuds out. I slowly open my mouth which feels and tastes of dried paste and hoarsely say, "I hate your music." Maggie bursts out laughing which incites an unwilling smile from me.

I *do* love her magical laugh. I always have. It trills on the air like music, and she has a way of bringing the pixie out of me. I don't remember ever getting into trouble until she learned how to walk and then, oh boy, we became impetuous imps. The first swear word I remember hearing was a time when Maggie was three and I was five. Thinking I was so mature I decided to show off my newly learned skill of lighting a match. I held it up proudly until the flame got too close to my fingers and I instinctively dropped it into a trash can full of paper. As the fire blossomed, so did our panic. Our screams of alarm brought our parents rushing from the other room. When Dad saw the flames, he said a word that set my ears aflame, and he ran to get the fire extinguisher. The memory of my fear combined with the looks of fear on our parents' faces would have been enough punishment to never do it again, but my parents decided I needed something more to help me remember.

As Dad doled out the punishment, he said the oddest thing, "This hurts me more than it hurts you."

"What?!" I thought. "Is he crazy? I'm pretty certain my backside hurts more than his hand." I know *now* that he meant emotional pain and not physical pain.

The door to my hospital room opens and Mom walks in carrying two sodas. She sees Maggie's beaming face and looks at me. She rushes to my side, and says, "I'm so glad you're finally awake! You sure like scaring me half to death, don't you?"

"It's good to see you too, Mom," I croak.

Mom sets the sodas on my bedside table and pushes it aside so she can sit on the edge of my bed. She leans over and covers my face with kisses just like she did when I was little. Part of me resists, feeling I'm much too old for such treatment, but the bigger part of me, the part that wins, loves it. Her kisses send warm, loving, feelings from the top of my head to my toes and I smile.

"How did the surgery go?" I ask.

Mom smiles and says, "Very well, the doctor said he's certain he got all of the tumor."

Maggie crawls into bed with me. "Oww!" I howl. Maggie! That hurts, be careful!"

"Oh, be quiet, you big baby and hand me the remote," she says.

"Maggie!" Mom scoldingly exclaims, "Stitches!". Once Maggie and I are situated and the pain has subsided, I enjoy her closeness. It's comforting. We watch TV snuggled close together until I fall asleep again. I'm vaguely aware of her climbing out of the bed, but I'm too groggy to make much sense of it. My dreams are ordinary, in fact I don't really remember much of what I dream. All I know is that I didn't dream of Jack.

I wake to the sound of the nurse opening the door. She pulls the curtain back and a shaft of light from the hallway intrudes across my room, bed and into my eyes. I squint at her as she wraps a blood pressure cuff around my arm. As the machine does its job, she takes my other vitals. I look around the dim room and see Mom sleeping in a lounge chair specially designed to fold out into a small bed for those who spend the night with their loved one.

Someone has brought her a pillow and blanket. I hear her softly snore as I scan the room for Maggie, but she's nowhere in sight.

"What time is it?" I ask the nurse.

"It's two in the morning," she says matter-of-factly and not so quietly. "How are you feeling?"

"Ok, I guess," I say and push myself up. I groan as pain throbs throughout my abdomen.

"Take it easy there. We don't want you to pop any stitches. Here," she says, handing me the controls to the bed. I take it and raise myself to a higher incline. I realize that sitting straight up is out of the question. "I'm going to give you something to ease the pain and help you sleep," she says. Taking the IV tube she pokes a syringe into the port and empties its contents into the saline solution flowing into my veins.

I realize I need to go to the bathroom and decide I'd better mention it while the nurse is still here. "I need to go to the bathroom," I tell her.

"You have a catheter in, so you don't need to get up to relieve yourself," she informs me. I nod slowly as sleep once again overtakes me. My dreams remain void of Jack, which saddens me.

For the next few days I sleep a lot. I can feel my body healing and growing stronger. By the end of the week, the nurse takes out the catheter and helps me to the bathroom. My legs feel like wet noodles, but each trip gets a little easier. They finally let me eat real food, but all of it is soft and tasteless – except the Jell-O, at least it's lime, my favorite.

A few more days pass and I'm eating regular food again, which has a little more taste to it, but it is still hospital food. Nevertheless, I'm grateful for it. Along with the food comes talk of me going home. This is very welcome news because I'm alone in my room, which is actually a double room and they have me on the furthest side, the farthest from the door. The custodial closet is right next to my room. I can hear the staff accessing their closet, but the curtain is always drawn around me so I can't see what is happening. More than once I mistook the sounds as someone coming into my room. It's driving me crazy! When I see the doctor next, I'll ask to go home where I know I'll heal faster.

"Hey, in valid," Maggie says when she comes into my room.

"In valid?" Mom asks.

"Yeah, you know invalid, in valid." Mom just rolls her eyes. Maggie climbs in bed with me again. Now, after a few days of healing it's less painful. She grabs the remote and quickly changes the channels trying to find something interesting to watch. As soon as she's settled on a show, she pushes the button on the bed controls to call the nurse. After some time, the nurse comes into the room to see what I need.

"Could you bring me some juice and cookies?" Maggie asks. The nurse stares at her for a moment then sighs and chuckles, shaking her head as she walks toward the door. She stops and turns to Mom when she hears her scolding Maggie.

"Maggie! This isn't a restaurant, and she is not your waitress."

"No, it's ok," the nurse says, then looks at me and Mom, and asks, "Would you two like anything?" We give her our orders and she disappears into the hallway. When she returns with our food she says, "I used to work in the pediatric ward. Those kids had me running circles bringing them juice, milk, cookies and chips. This is nothing compared to that, so don't even worry about it." She pauses as she reaches the door, turns to us and says, "If you need anything else, just let me know."

"Thaaannkk yooouuu!" Maggie sings to the nurse between slurps from her juice box.

A short while later Dr. Jolly comes into the room. "Well, hello there," she says to Mom. "I talked with my brother Chris last night. He asked me to tell you hello."

"Oh, how is he doing?"

"He and his wife are doing very well. They're living in Washington, the Tri-Cities area. He's an electrical engineer who makes weapons of mass destruction. It's ironic that I work every day to save lives and he works every day to take lives." There's a pregnant pause as we all take in the images she's conjured up.

What a killjoy, I think.

"Well, your scans all look good," Dr. Jolly says. "And your incision is healing nicely as well. I'm giving the green light to go home."

"Yippee!" Maggie yells. "I'm getting really tired of this hospital food."

I give her a withering look and say, "Seriously?"

She shrugs her shoulders and says, "Well?"

"Vicki from my office will be calling you tomorrow to schedule a follow-up appointment for next week," Dr. Jolly says. Then she directs her next comment to Maggie, "I expect you to take good care of your sister." Maggie looks at her wide-eyed and nods her head.

On our way home, we stop at the pharmacy to pick up the pain meds the doctor prescribed. Maggie opts to stay in the car with me. I know it's so she can watch over me because Maggie's not one to pass up an opportunity to buy herself her favorite candy, M&M's.

I groan a little as I shift in my seat. Maggie's attention snaps to me, "Are you okay?" she asks, sounding near panic.

"I'm fine," I say, trying not to let my irritation sound in my voice. She's taking this assignment from the doctor way too seriously. Maggie relaxes and turns her attention back to her phone. She smiles as she reads a text. My curiosity supersedes my manners and I ask, "Who's texting you?"

Maggie stops, looking frozen. I can see the wheels in her brain whirling. Obviously, she doesn't feel comfortable telling me. A moment later she says, trying to sound carefree, "Just a friend."

"Oh, anyone I know?" There again is that deer in the headlights look. That's when I realize she's not hiding it because she's embarrassed. She's hiding something *from* me. Now I'm somewhere between 'curiosity killed the cat' and 'I'm going to strangle you'. I grab for her phone but the effort of it makes my belly hurt. I wince and cry out with pain.

"Jenn!" Maggie cries. "What hurts? Should I go get Mom?" she asks, concern oozing from her. I shake my head and take a deep breath letting it out slowly.

"I'm fine now," I lie. I discreetly hold my incision so Maggie won't see and freak out again. Mom comes back and we're on our way home.

I walk into the family room which is adjacent to the kitchen. I walk past the couch, recliners, around the corner and into my bedroom. I lie down and sigh. It feels good to be home, sleeping in my own bed without nurses waking me up several times in the middle of the night. I stare up at the ceiling and make out the shape of ships in the texturing, thinking of Jack. I'm a bit afraid to admit that I'm worried I won't dream about him anymore. I close my eyes hoping I'll fall asleep, but after an hour sleep still evades me. I smell something cooking and decide to go find out what Mom is making for dinner. I round the corner into the living room and see Maggie on the couch with the TV on and she's crocheting.

Crocheting? When did she learn to do that and why? I wonder. I can tell by the way she is struggling it's a new hobby. I gingerly sit next to her and silently watch. "When did you take up crocheting?" I ask, causing her to jump. "Sorry, I didn't mean to scare you," I say.

"That's ok," she says, laying her crocheting in her lap, her fingers still entwined in the yarn. "Well, I've been interested in taking it up for a while. When Hunter was here, he said something about how his mom crochets and well…" she pauses as a blush creeps up her cheeks, "well…it inspired me to go ahead and start."

"Oh, I see," I say. It's very clear to me now that she has feelings for Hunter. I know I should be jealous, but for some reason I find it sweet. I haven't been dating Hunter for very long and I realize now I'm really not all that into him.

Besides, I have Jack now, I think. *Wait! What?* The thought that I even think of Jack as more than a figment of my imagination shocks me. I gasp which sets Maggie off.

"What's wrong?" she asks with that panic in her voice again.

I bite my bottom lip and shake my head. She eyes me warily before she eases back into her seat. "If you need anything just let me know," she says.

I smile and say, "I know." I contemplate telling her about my dreams and about Jack but decide against it.

She'd probably think I'm off my rocker, I think. I turn my attention toward the TV hoping to distract myself.

We spend the rest of the evening together, watching one sitcom after another, only stopping long enough to eat the delicious dinner Mom makes for us. Unfortunately, my stomach can't hold much of it which earns me a worried look from Mom.

That night as I snuggle into bed, I wonder if, no…I *hope* I dream of Jack. I whisper a short prayer with the hope that God will make it happen. With that prayer still on my lips, I fall asleep.

We stand at our usual spot on the outcrop of rock. Our hands are intertwined. I squeeze his and smile. Giggling, I let go and scamper down the rock without any pain, feeling free for the first time in a while. I sit on a log to remove my shoes and stockings. As I approach the water's edge, I gather my long skirt up around my knees and plunge my feet into the refreshing water. Mesmerized, I watch as the frothy water splashes my ankles and shins. Jack's shadow falls across me and I feel his presence just behind me. I turn to look at him and see that the early morning sun behind him frames him and sets him aglow. A sigh escapes me, and I can't help thinking he looks like a god.

"Shall we walk?" he asks.

"I'd like that," I say and step out of the waves. I grab my shoes and fall in step with Jack. We walk until my impish side starts to take over and I have this uncontrollable urge to tease him. I snatch Jack's hat from his head, loving the way his curls topple out of it and around his ears.

"Hey!" he objects and reaches for it. I turn and run down the beach laughing. "Why you little minx!" he shouts and chases after me. It doesn't take long for him to catch up, but of course I want him to catch me. I stop running, breathing heavily, dangling his hat out to my side.

"Please give me my hat," he laughs, holding his hand out. Giggling I put it behind me, flashing him my most coquettish smile. He walks around me hoping to snatch it back, but like the moon, I turn with him, always keeping my face toward him. Frustrated, he growls and quickly reaches around me. Suddenly he stops, very aware of how close we are. I can feel his breath on my cheek. We study each other's eyes for a moment, then his eyes move to my lips and my heart beats wildly.

With each beat my heart calls out to him, begging him, *Kiss me. Boom, boom. Kiss me! Boom, boom. KISS ME!* I close my eyes anticipating the touch of his lips. But then he pulls away. My eyes snap open. He's walking away! I stand stunned, watching his back as he walks away from me. Disappointed and confused, I put on his hat pulling it down over my ears. It smells like him, a mixture of salt and leather. Scowling, I follow him down the beach. I wake the next morning feeling grumpy.

Chapter 6 Chemotherapy

I tremble as Mom pulls into the parking lot of the Pacific Northwest Cancer Treatment Center. It's my first day of chemo. My "bring it on" attitude got me through the surgery, but it isn't working for me today. It could have something to do with the feeling that I'm about to have rat poison pumped through my body.

The building is squat and sprawls out across the asphalt as if Godzilla had taken a skyscraper from New York City, smashed it like a banana and transplanted it to the west coast. It seems old, most likely due to the fact that it has additions upon additions. The crisp, dark red walls of the main part of the building are now faded. Attached to the north side is a newer wing painted an orange, rust color. It coordinates well with the faded red. All I can see of the rest of the building is the end of it. It appears to make an "L" shape off the back of the main building.

Mom and I walk to the entrance. As we approach the glass doors, they slide open automatically with a hiss. Warm air spills out and quickly engulfs us. It feels delightful and helps calm my jittery nerves a little. The reception area is spacious and just inside the door is a long counter where we check in. We approach it and the receptionist greets us, hands me some forms to fill out, takes our insurance information, and asks us to sit in the waiting area. There's a grouping of metal framed chairs covered in subdued, blue fabric. We find two seats together and sit. Mom helps me fill out the forms.

I discreetly look around the room. The teal-colored walls sport paintings of peaceful landscapes. No doubt to help calm the patients and those who're with them. Several hallways branch off of the waiting area leading to exam rooms, doctor's offices, radiology, and infusion rooms. I look around at our fellow patients waiting with us. They're from all walks of life, genders, and ages.

I guess cancer is non-discriminatory, I think. It's easy to distinguish those who're currently undergoing treatment from those who're not. Their bald heads and gaunt faces give them away. Some hide their baldness with some kind of head covering, while others just let it all hang out.

I overhear a little boy around four talking to an elderly man sitting next to him. As he runs his hand over his little bald head he says, "Dis is my chiwy haiw." I have to think for a moment before I understand he's saying chilly hair.

How dang cute is that? I think. My heart breaks as I think of how hard it must be to go through this at his age. He just wants to be a typical kid and play and have a worry-free life. It seems so unfair to burden him with all this. I watch his mother as she interacts with him. She wears a haunted look. One that speaks of long-worrisome nights followed by worrisome days – always wondering if this day will be the last day with her son. I imagine this must be how a soldier at war looks. Constantly at battle. Constantly wondering if today will be his last sunrise, his last meal, his last breath?

That would be so hard to deal with, I think, but then I realize I *am* dealing with it. I shiver.

"Are you cold?" Mom asks and rubs my arms.

"I'm fine," I say, but I'm not. A ball of panic grows inside me, and I can't sit still anymore. I stand up and walk around. As I circle around the back of the waiting room, I see a table set up with an assortment of juices, bottled water, and coffee.

I pass on the coffee thinking; *I'm already wound up enough as it is. Coffee will probably send me spinning like a Whirling Dervish.* I pick an apple juice and drink as I lean against the wall. I can't seem to keep my eyes off the little boy and his mother. There's something almost magical about them. I don't think I've ever seen a parent-child bond like theirs before. She looks at him as if he's her masterpiece and her mentor all rolled into one. I walk back to my chair. I take Mom's hand and just quietly hold it. Surprised, she looks at me and smiles. I don't look at her, but I feel her gaze and a smile creeps across my lips. All too soon, I hear my name. I sigh. Hesitantly, we get up and walk to the nurse waiting at the entrance to the chemo hallway and follow her.

We stop at a desk just outside the infusion room to verify who I am and that I'm in the right place. From there we walk past three small rooms with beds. One of them holds a patient, sleeping as medically approved poison slowly flows into her body. We move to a large oval shaped room. White vinyl recliners line both sides of the room. Many of which are occupied by my fellow patients. I see my name on a white board sitting on a table next to a recliner.

"Here we go," the nurse says. She motions for me to sit down. I take a deep breath trying to calm my fears and shakily sit down. Chairs flank each recliner; Mom takes the one next to mine. There's also a small table next to the recliner. I look at the man next to me. He seems to be about my age, maybe a little older. A young woman sits with him. By the look of their matching facial features, I feel certain she's his sister. They're putting a jigsaw puzzle together, listening to music on a laptop and talking. I correct myself, it's more like they're bantering.

I settle back into my chair and the nurse shows me how to adjust it to maximize my comfort. She brings me a pillow and a heated blanket. I guess she noticed my quivering. The warmth of the blanket seeps into my body, helping to calm my nerves.

The phone on the wall rings and my nurse answers it. She talks to the person on the other end for a few minutes then says, "Yes. I'll send her right up." When she hangs up, she approaches and says, "Sandra, they need you up front to sort out an insurance issue."

"Will you be okay?" she asks me.

"We'll take good care of her. She'll be just fine," the nurse says. Mom nods, gets up and walks out.

The nurse disappears and comes back a few minutes later with a bag of fluid. It's a clear liquid and the bag is marked saline. "This is just a saline solution to flush your PICC line," she says as she fiddles with the plastic tubing that will deliver the saline into my body. I unbutton the middle button of my blouse and pull out the tubing that protrudes from just under my sternum. When the doctor did my operation, he also implanted the PICC line. The nurse then attaches the tubing from the saline solution to my PICC line. She puts a hand on my shoulder, looks me in the face and says, "I'll be right back." I nod and watch her walk across the room and disappear into another room. She's gone long enough for the saline bag to empty into my veins. I try to wait patiently but the beeping of the IV machine is driving me crazy. I look around for a nurse or someone who works here who could either stop the beeping or find someone who could, but no one is in sight. My next tactic is to turn the machine around and try to turn it off myself, but I can't quite reach it. I start to struggle out of my recliner.

"Here, let me help," the sister sitting next to me says. She turns the IV pole toward me and shows me which button to push to silence the beeping. "It only stays silent for about fifteen minutes. You can keep pushing it until the nurse comes back."

I smile and say, "Thanks." After pushing the button, I lean back into the seat.

"My name is Piper," the sister says. "And this is my brother, Alex." Alex salutes in my direction.

"Nice to meet you. I'm Jenn," I say.

"First time?" Alex asks. I nod. "Leukemia," he says. "And you?"

"Stomach," I say mimicking the abbreviated way he speaks. "How...how long have you had cancer," I ask.

"Too long," he says, looking disgruntled.

"This is his second bout with leukemia," Piper adds. "He first had leukemia when he was a junior in high school. They thought they'd cured it and it was in remission for about ten years. Then last year it came back." She looks over at her brother, drawing my attention to him. He's sitting with his chin resting on his fist, staring out the window. I'm not certain he's even listening but there's a look of pain on his face.

Mom comes back and says as she sits down, "All done now." The nurse returns a few moments later dressed in a protective gown and gloves, carrying an IV bag labeled with a bright orange sticker that says, 'hazardous chemo'. My stomach knots up when I see her attach it to my IV pole. I want to vomit already, and the chemotherapy hasn't even hit my system. "Make sure you drink lots of fluids to protect your kidneys," the nurse tells me as she replaces the saline with the bag of chemo and attaches it to my PICC line. "There are restrooms there, there, and over there," she says looking very much like a stewardess pointing out all the emergency exits. She also tells me what is available to drink: a plethora of juices and electrolyte ladened power drinks. When the nurse leaves, I see Piper out of the corner of my eye lean over to Mom and touch my arm. I unintentionally flinch.

"It's not so bad at first," she says.

I want to say, "And how would *you* know?" but I hold my tongue because I know she means well. I sit back and try not to think about the poison flowing into my body.

Alex turns to me, gives me an encouraging smile and a thumbs up. I nod, close my eyes, and try not think about the horrible things the chemo is doing to my body. Hoping I can pass the four to five hours I'll be here by dreaming about Jack, I allow myself to start to drift off. Suddenly, there's a crash close by. My eyes fly open to see a man setting up a keyboard across the room from me. He looks to be in his early 70's, his white hair betraying his age. He's wearing a blue Hawaiian shirt, a lei around his neck and a snorkel/goggle set strapped to his forehead. I guess he's going for a luau theme. I watch, somewhat amused as he sets up his equipment. It takes him a few tries, but he finally gets everything set up. He runs his fingers up and down the keys a couple of times and then begins to play and sing the song *Tiny Bubbles* which is followed by a number of other Hawaiian themed songs. He then opens the floor for requests. When no one responds, I look around and see that the infusion room is a beehive of activity. Nurses scurry around taking patients' blood pressures, temperatures, weights, getting them blankets and in general making them as comfortable as possible.

Mom pipes up and requests an old '80's song. The man smiles and immediately begins performing it. I want to laugh, but then realize if I do, I just might wet my pants. I touch Mom's arm and ask, "Would you help me to the bathroom?"

"Of course," she says. I quickly scope out all the bathrooms and decide on one, but as I'm getting out of the chair someone else goes in. I aim for a different one, but as I'm nearing the door another person slips inside. I quickly change course and finally make it to a recently vacated bathroom. Mom comes in with me and helps me manage the IV machine and tubing. As I finish up, I hear a soft knock on the door. Obviously, these rooms are in high demand.

As I return to my recliner, the man with the keyboard is packing up his equipment. "Thank you for entertaining us," Mom says to the man.

His smile beams. "You are very welcome," he says with a little bow. "I've been in your shoes before."

"Oh?" Mom says, inviting him to share his story.

"My wife had breast cancer and we spent many long days here. I just thought if I performed music for you, it might make it a little easier."

"Let your wife know we appreciate her sparing you today to come entertain us," Mom says.

The man's smile turns sad, and he says, his eyes twinkling with moisture, "Unfortunately, my wife didn't make it."

"Oh, I'm so sorry. I'm always saying the wrong thing."

The man shakes his head and says, "Don't worry about it. I don't mind sharing. Although I miss her terribly, death is just part of life. We're born dying and who knows, I could walk out of here and die on my way home." Mom looks at him like she might cry then helps him pack up the last of his equipment. She comes over and sits down as the man leaves, watching him thoughtfully as he walks away. Both Mom and I then pull out our phones and engross ourselves in social media. Before too long I feel the need to relieve myself again.

I look at Mom and say, "I need to go again."

"Already?" she asks. "Ok. Well, let's get going before they're all filled." We make it to the closest bathroom before someone else can snatch it.

We spend the next three hours like this, entertaining ourselves between bathroom breaks. Finally, the last bag of chemo is done, and the nurse comes to hook up a bag of saline solution, and...I have to go again. I feel as if I'm spending more time in the bathroom than in my recliner. When the saline is done the nurse unhooks the IV and sends us home with the promise of more chemo tomorrow.

When we walk into the house it's quiet. There's a note on the table which says, "I got called into work. I should be home by 6. I made enchiladas. They're in the fridge. I hope you like them but remember to save me some. Love you, Maggie." As Mom gets the enchiladas out of the fridge and warms them up, I wonder when I'll start feeling the effects of the chemo. I go to the computer and start researching. After a half hour Mom calls me to the table. She's added homemade guacamole, yum, sour cream, tortilla chips and some of her famous homemade salsa to the enchiladas. My mouth starts watering as I sit down to eat.

After saying grace, we dish up and begin to talk. "I was doing some research just now and the general consensus is that I'll start feeling the effects of the chemo in about a month," I say. "People suggest that by cutting my hair short now, before it starts to fall out, it will cut back on all the long hair all over the place. They also say it helps with the transition."

Mom sighs heavily, blinks a couple of times and says, "That's quite a pragmatic approach to this." She nods then continues, "Do you want me to make an appointment at the salon?"

I run my hands through my hair a few times trying to decide whether I should do it or not. I know it's probably a wise thing to do but, I just can't bring myself to do it. "No," I say. "I'm not quite ready to part with it yet. But thanks for offering,"

After dinner I go to the family room and watch some TV in an attempt to get my mind on something else. During a quiet conversation in the movie, I can hear Mom in her room, sobbing. My heart breaks for her and I want to go to her to apologize for it all, but I know it could never take away the pain. Feeling helpless, I do the only thing I can think of. I mute the TV and kneel on the floor and talk to God.

"Dear Father, it's me again. I think this is a record. This is the most I've talked to you, ever. I hope you don't mind me asking you for more stuff. My mom's really sad right now. She lost my dad a long time ago and now I'm sick. I think she's afraid I might die too. Heck, I'm afraid of that myself. This is all so hard. Could you please help us with this? I know you're busy and all, but we could really use your help. Thank you. In the name of Jesus Christ, Amen."

Just as I finish my prayer the doorbell rings. I get up, walk to the door, and open it. To my surprise Dr. Hunky is standing there with a bouquet of flowers in his hand. "Hello," he says with a dashing smile. "Is Sandy home?"

"Yeah. Come in," I say, showing him into the living room. "Have a seat and I'll go get her." He perches nervously on the edge of the sofa while I go to Mom's room. I knock softly on the door. She calls for me to come in. I open the door and see her lying on the bed, hugging her pillow. "Mom, Dr. Pearson is here to see you."

Her head pops up and she looks at me surprised. Then her eyes narrow and she says dryly, "Ha, ha. Funny joke."

I start to laugh and say, "Mom, I'm not joking. He really is here. Come see for yourself."

She gets up and walks toward the door, pausing for a moment to check her reflection. After wiping the mascara from beneath her eyes and adjusting some of the locks of her hair that had fallen from her barrette, she walks down the hall. "This better not be one of your jokes," she hisses. I hear a slight gasp when she turns the corner and sees Dr. Hunky sitting there in real life. "H-hello Scott. This is a surprise."

He jumps to his feet and walks across the room to meet her, looking like a nervous teenager going on his first date. "Hi Sandy," he says. Mom giggles. He then hands her the bouquet of flowers and states, "These are for you."

"Thank you. They're beautiful," she says and takes the flowers and smells them. "I should put these in some water," she says as she turns toward the kitchen.

"I'll take them, Mom. You stay here and visit," I say, taking the flowers from her. As I search for a vase, fill it with water and place the flowers in it, I hear them talking. I can't make out what they're saying, but I hope it's not about me and cancer related things. I hope it's getting-to-know-you stuff. I take the vase of flowers into the living room and set them on the table in front of the sofa where she can admire them while they visit.

"Oh, thank you, Sweetheart," Mom says.

"You're welcome," I say, catching her eye. She flashes me a smile full of wonderment and a little giggle escapes her mouth. I try to suppress my own laugh and quickly excuse myself. About an hour into their visit, I hear Maggie's car pull into the garage.

When she comes in, she says too loudly, "Whose car is that out front? Do we have company?"

I shush her, grab her arm, and pull her back into the garage. "It's *Dr. Hunky*! He's here to see Mom."

"What?!" Maggie asks. I nod my head vigorously confirming that I spoke the truth. "Mom's dating?"

"I really hope so. She needs a good distraction."

We creep into the house, across the family room and peek around the corner to spy on them. She's smiling radiantly. I suddenly see her as a young woman, beautiful, vivacious, and charismatic, and I understand why Dr.

Hunky might be attracted to her. We can't hear most of their conversation, but then they stand and walk to the door. He takes her hand, gently kisses it, and says, "I'll see you tomorrow night then, at 7." He bids her goodnight and leaves. I hear a loud sigh below me. I look down and see Maggie looking all dreamy.

Mom's head pops up and her eyes fly open when she sees us there. "Have you two been spying on us the whole time?"

"Isn't he dreamy, Mom?" Maggie says as she straightens and walks toward her. She takes Mom's hands in hers and holds them high above them. She twirls Mom under her arm then she ducks under Mom's arm.

Mom starts to laugh and says, "Yes, he *is* very dreamy and he's taking me to dinner tomorrow night."

"Tomorrow?" Maggie says. I can't contain the squeal that bursts from me, and I start to dance around, followed by Maggie. We dance around Mom until I'm exhausted, and I fall onto the sofa. I sit there and watch Mom and Maggie continue to dance. This day couldn't have had a better ending.

Chapter 7 The Big Date

It feels like Deja vu as we walk into the treatment center today. Maggie has the day off from work so she can help Mom get ready for her date. She came to my chemo appointment with me this time because she was worried that if Mom were to come, she'd get too tired or depressed to go on her date. We don't want anything stopping Mom from going out and enjoying herself. There's very little that Maggie remembers about Dad because she was so young when he died. She's had to watch Mom be alone for almost her entire life.

As soon as I'm settled into my recliner, a nurse comes and starts the whole process again. She hooks me up to the IV, gives me a pillow and blanket, and takes our lunch orders. I realize this will be the pattern of my life for the next five months – one full week of chemo, then two weeks off, then back to the chemo. The thought makes me want to curl up and wither away. But then Maggie's delightful laugh entices me away from my misery.

"Watch this," she demands, shoving her phone in my face. I watch a short video of a puppy as it encounters stairs for the first time. The video elicits a chuckle from me. I hand the phone back to her. A few moments later she's laughing again and shoving her phone in my face to watch another video. This one's of a toddler shoving things into his underpants. The rest of the morning continues along this same vein, Maggie laughing at a video and forcing me to watch it. By the time lunch arrives, I'm beyond ready for a break from video watching. At times, I go to the bathroom when I don't really need to, just to give myself a break.

When the nurse comes to take away our lunch trays, I ask Maggie if we can do something different this afternoon. She grins mischievously and pulls a *Gentlemen's Quarterly* out of her purse. Leaning in real close she whispers, "We're going to ogle good looking men." With a wicked laugh, she opens the magazine and starts perusing all the pictures. She holds it so I can see it as well, but I can't muster enough interest to pay attention.

Without even realizing it, I fall asleep and find myself standing on the rock on the beach. Jack is by my side and we're holding hands again, but this time I quickly drop his hand, feeling a little frosty after my attempt to get him to kiss me was snubbed. I climb down and start walking toward the town. I'm not sure if Jack is following me or not. I start to look back but stop, reminding myself that I don't care. When I reach the steps to the town, I hear Jack panting behind. He obviously had to run to catch up to me. A small smile threatens to burst out on my face, but I quickly keep it in check.

"Why are you in such a hurry?" he asks between attempts to catch his breath. I just shrug my shoulders and start climbing.

When we get to the top of the steps, we're both panting. I stop to catch my breath. With my hand on my waist I look around for something to do. My eyes land on an ancient oak tree and I walk to it and say, "I want to climb this tree." I reach between my ankles, grab the back of my skirt, pull it up between my legs and tuck it into my belt. Out of the corner of my eye I see Jack fixing me with a bewildered look.

I look at him and say, "What?" He points to my skirt. I look down, then back at him and do a little swish with my hips. "Instant pants," I say, and Jack's hearty laugh rumbles in my chest. I wrap my hands around a low hanging branch and try to climb the tree. I first pull myself up and try to sling my leg around the branch, but all I manage to do is catch my foot on the branch. My foot quickly slides off. I try again and again but never get any further than almost pulling my shoe off as my foot slides off the branch. I circle the tree searching for a better way to get up but come back to the original spot. I look up at the tree feeling defeated and internally growling at Jack. Part of me wants him to help me but I am too proud to ask and too proud to let him help me. I decide to give it one more try, determined to do it all by myself. This time I actually get my knee around the branch but can't manage to go any further. I dangle there for a moment, then try to hoist myself up onto the top of the branch. As I struggle, I feel Jack's hands on my waist. All my frosty thoughts and feelings melt away with the warmth of his touch.

As if I'm made of feathers, he hoists me up onto the top of the branch. From there I get my footing and I easily scramble up into the "Y" of the tree. I turn to help Jack up. But he doesn't need my help. With animal-like agility he easily bounds up the tree. Once he's situated on the other side of the "Y" from me, he notices the stunned look on my face.

"What?" he asks.

"Are you part cheetah?" I ask.

He chuckles, thinking for a moment and says, "No, I guess from all that time as a sailor…climbing the rigging and all, it made it easy to climb trees."

"Yeah, I suppose that would do it." I lean back against the branch across from him and look around. To my right I see the beach where we always meet. To my left I see the hall where we attended the concert and the ice cream parlor down the street. With the intention of turning around to see what else I can see from this vantage point, I push myself upright, and lose my balance. I try to right myself but instead I fall into Jack. Our bodies smashed up against each other, I can feel his heart beating and his warm breath against my cheek. His arm snakes around my waist, steadying me.

"I'm so sorry," I say and push against him to separate myself from him, but his arm remains tight around me.

"May I kiss you?" he breathes.

"You don't have to ask," I say.

"Yes, I do. A gentleman always asks first," he whispers.

"Well then. Yes, you may kiss me."

"Thank you," he says and closing the distance between us, his lips tenderly kiss mine. Then he kisses me again, deeper this time as if trying to drink in my very essence. I thread my arms around him and pull him tight, trying to fuse our bodies together. When our lips finally part he says, "I've been wanting to do that for so long."

I look at him puzzled and say, "If you wanted to kiss me, why didn't you do it the other day when I stole your hat?"

He looks a little sheepish and says, "I wanted to, but I was afraid."

"Afraid?" I ask incredulously. "Afraid of what?"

He bows his head looking ashamed and says, "I was afraid that if I kissed you then, I wouldn't be satisfied with just a kiss."

I don't know what to say to comfort him. I look at his bowed head for a moment thinking. Then I hook my finger under his chin and lift it. When our eyes meet, I say, "Thank you for valuing my virtue." I lean in and softly kiss him on the cheek. He touches his cheek where I kissed it, then touches his lips as if trying to transfer it to his mouth.

I hear someone giggling, which gives me the sense that I'm being laughed at. I struggle to open my eyes. I feel them fluttering, but I can't get them open. I hear the giggling again. Now I'm mad. With all my might I force my eyes open and see Maggie looking at her phone and laughing. With a smile as big as the Grand Canyon, she composes a text. Now I'm really mad. I want to reach up and tear the phone from her, but I don't have the energy. Instead, I stare daggers into her. Finally, she looks at me and somewhat surprised says, "Oh! You're awake."

"Yes," I hiss through gritted teeth, "no thanks to you."

"Whoa, girlfriend. What's got your panties in a wad?" she asks. I consider giving her a piece of my mind, but decide I better just let it go or I might have to tell her about Jack. I sit up straighter in my seat and catch a glimpse of the clock. It's almost 3:00. I look at the bag of chemo and see it's almost done. The thought of curling up in my own bed and sleeping for a week sounds so appealing.

"Don't give in to your fatigue," the woman next to me says.

I look at her. She seems to be in her late sixties and has that, "this is not my first chemotherapy rodeo" air about her. I ask, "Why do you say that?"

She leans closer and says, "Because, if you stop moving while you're on chemo, you'll never get moving again." I nod my understanding.

Her chestnut wig lies abandoned on her side table. It reminds me of my neighbor's Shih Tzu dogs. I half expect it to jump up and run away barking. There are bright red spots on her scalp where the wig has irritated her skin. Looking at them makes me cringe and I wonder if that will happen to me too.

Before I can ask the woman any more questions, my nurse approaches and begins to flush my line with saline solution. I expect to smell a salty, sea scent but instead I smell lemons and rubbing alcohol.

Odd, I think. "Maybe the chemo is messing with my senses." Just then someone walks in carrying a bag of food from my favorite burger place. I expect to feel hungry when I smell it but instead it triggers nausea. In the blink of an eye, my lunch vaults from my stomach and all over my legs. Surprised, Maggie jumps up and screams as if she'd seen a mouse. The nurse, who had just walked away, races back with an emesis basin (a.k.a. a barf bucket). She rubs my back, talking to me soothingly as I face down into the bucket, and let it all go. I stay that way as I wait for my stomach to calm down. I notice out of the corner of my eye a woman standing next to me with a bucket and mop waiting to clean up the mess. Another nurse brings me some drab pink scrubs to change into and walks with me to the bathroom where she helps me change my clothes. My legs shake and I worry they might give out on me. I'm grateful for everyone's help, but it all makes me feel like a child again.

As I sit back in my freshly cleaned seat, the woman with the Shih Tzu-like wig says to me, "Don't worry, Honey. We've all been there. A few years ago when I was here for my first treatments, a young man threw up. Soon, it set off a chain reaction that had half the patients here barfing. You should have seen those nurses fly! I think the whole housekeeping staff was here," she says chuckling.

The nurse who'd returned to unhook my tubes said, "We count it a good day when we only have one person vomit."

I look at Maggie to see if she's getting ready to go. Her face is pale, and she looks as if she might faint. The nurse runs and grabs some smelling salts. She cracks them open and puts them below Maggie's nose. Maggie jumps and shakes her head. The nurse looks at me and mouths, "Bring someone else next time." I nod my agreement.

Maggie insists on giving Mom and me mani/pedis to help each of us feel more girly. I figure it's a good idea since, in a short while, all my hair is going to fall out and I'm not going to feel like anything but a big blob of human flesh.

When our nails are dry, I lie on Mom's bed admiring the pretty polish and watch Maggie help Mom decide what to wear for her date.

"It's been so long since I've been on a date. I'm not sure how to dress or act," Mom says, sounding near panic.

"Just take a deep breath, Mom. It's not rocket science and besides, it's probably been a long time for him too." Mom looks thoughtful for a moment, nods her head, inhales deeply, holds it for a second, then lets it out slowly – letting her shoulders relax as she does.

"Ok, I'm better now. Let's pick out a dress. Or should I wear pants?" There was that panic again.

"Mom! Relax!" Maggie exclaims, looking her in the eyes. She grabs Mom's shoulders and starts doing deep breathing exercises. Mom quickly follows.

This is better than anything on TV, I think with a giggle.

Maggie dives into Mom's closet several times, emerging each time with a different outfit. Each one Mom tries on and models for us. As she parades around, we give her our opinions. Sometimes Maggie goes and retrieves accessories to go with the outfit. After a few turns around the room we always come to the consensus that it's not the right dress.

"What I need is a little black dress," Mom says. This sparks a memory.

"Maggie, in the back of my closet is the dress I wore for Annie's wedding. I think it just might be what we're looking for," I say. Maggie grins and goes to retrieve the dress. A few minutes later she returns with it. A flimsy, transparent, plastic bag covers it, a 'gift' from the dry cleaners. Maggie pulls it off to reveal a short, black, form fitting, lace dress.

"I'll never fit into that!" she says, slapping her belly.

"Just try it, Mom. You might be pleasantly surprised," I say.

"Yeah, Mom, try it on," Maggie agrees. Mom reluctantly grabs the dress, looks at it dubiously, and as she walks into the bathroom, she shakes her head.

Maggie and I wait on the bed with great anticipation, nervously holding each other's hands. We listen to the swish of fabric and the zip of the zipper, then silence. "Come on, Mom! Let us see," Maggie calls.

"Yeah, Mom, don't keep us waiting," I add.

A few seconds of silence, then she emerges from the bathroom. Maggie and I gasp simultaneously.

"Mom! You look gorgeous!" Maggie exclaims.

"Dr. Hunky's not going to be able to keep his eyes off of you. Actually, I think it looks better on you than it ever did on me," I say.

"Really?" she asks, examining herself in the mirror. She turns sideways, puts her hand on her stomach and sucks it in. "I don't know. My stomach pokes out a lot."

"Some Spanx will fix that," Maggie says.

Mom looks at her alarmed, puts her hands on her hips and says, "No one will be spanking any one around here!"

Giggling, Maggie says, "Mom, Spanx is like a girdle."

"Oooh," she replies and chuckles, looking sheepish.

"I have a pair," Maggie says, jumping off the bed and running to her room. She returns a few moments later waving a black pair in her hand. "Try these on," she says. Mom examines them skeptically. Finally, she shrugs her shoulders and slips them on under the dress. With a wiggle, a couple of jumps and a shimmy they're finally on.

Mom examines her now slimmer image in the mirror.

"Wow!" she exclaims. "These are miracle undies. I need to get myself some."

I lie back on the bed and watch as Maggie helps Mom do her makeup and hair and wonder if I'll ever be able to do those kinds of activities again. My attention is ripped from my thoughts when Mom asks, "What do you think, Jenn?"

I look up and see a version of Mom that I thought only existed in old family photos. "Mom, you look beautiful," I say.

"Really?" she asks, examining herself in the mirror, not sure I'm telling her the entire truth.

Maggie squeals with delight, clapping her hands gleefully. She takes Mom's hand and starts dancing around her singing, "Mommy's got a daaate, a daaate. She's gonna come home laaate. Dr. Hunky's gonna like her, maybe even kiss her."

"Maggie!" Mom exclaims. "We haven't even been on the date yet. Please, no more talk of kissing or I might get too nervous and back out." Maggie immediately stops and pulls an imaginary zipper across her lips.

Mom gathers her sweater and purse, and we all move to the living room to wait. She sits rigidly on the couch. The only movement is her rapidly bouncing leg. Maggie kneels on the couch and twists the plastic rod, opening the blinds just enough for her to keep watch. It brings back memories of when we were kids and she'd do the same thing while waiting for a friend to arrive. I sit across the room and smile as I watch the two of them and their entertaining display of nervousness.

Mom jumps when Maggie announces, "He's here!" She then plasters on a smile that almost looks convincing. Maggie rushes to the door and opens it just as he rings the doorbell. There stands Dr. Hunky in all his handsomeness, looking as nervous as Mom.

She walks to the door and says weakly, "Hi, Scott. Would you like to come in?"

He smiles shyly, nods and steps into the house.

Maggie closes the door behind him and mouths, "WOW!" and fans herself as if his gorgeousness is making her overheat. I try hard to contain my laughter, but I doubt Dr. Hunky can even take his eyes off Mom.

"You look beautiful, Sandy," he says, causing Mom to blush in a pretty way.

"You know Jennifer, but have you met my other daughter, Maggie?" Mom asks, motioning to her to come to her side. Dr. Hunky reluctantly tears his eyes from Mom and looks at Maggie. He extends his hand, she takes it, and they exchange niceties. After which, his attention is immediately drawn, as if by a magnet, back to Mom.

"Shall we go?" he asks. She agrees, and before we know it, he's whisked her away. As the door closes behind them, I'm struck with an acute feeling of loss, almost like I'm losing my mommy to him. I fight the urge to run to the door and call them back, but I know I would look ridiculous. I have to let her go. I wonder if this is how parents feel when their children grow up and go out on their own.

"Let's go watch some TV," I say, wanting something to distract me from this horrid feeling. Maggie doesn't say anything; she only walks silently into the family room. As we settle onto the couch, Maggie begins clicking through the channels. A few shows come on that look mildly entertaining, but she doesn't stay on any of them for very long.

Finally, she turns to me and says, "I feel kind of funny inside, like I'm sending off a kindergartener to go slay a dragon."

"I feel the same way," I say.

"Is this normal? Is there something wrong with Mom dating? Or is there something wrong with us?" she asks.

"I don't know," I begin, "I guess since we've had Mom to ourselves for all these years it would make sense that it would be a little hard to share her with someone else."

Maggie thinks for a few minutes then nods her head and says, "Yeah, that makes sense. How did you get so smart?"

I shrug my shoulders and say, laughing, "I don't know. Let's watch something funny to get our minds off it." With that I snatch the remote from her and scroll through the channels again to find a comedy. We settle on a movie and Maggie goes to the kitchen to make some popcorn. We laugh, we cry, we eat popcorn.

It's 10:45 and Mom is not home yet. I want to stay awake until she gets back but I can't keep my eyes open. My eyelids slide closed and I'm on our rock; Jack takes me by the hand and helps me down.

"Do you like to dance?" he asks as he leads me toward the stairs into town.

"I do," I say thinking of all the school dances and night clubs I've attended.

"Good, because I'm taking you to the town dance," he says. We ascend the stairs and emerge across from the park. We walk toward the same hall where we attended the concert. The doors are flung open, and I can hear people chatting, whooping, and laughing. Music pours from the hall but it's the kind of music you square dance to. We walk into the hall and see people twirling, sashaying to and fro, do-si-doing around the room. A man stands on the platform with the band, calling out the moves for the couples to make.

"Um, Jack, I haven't danced like this since I was in sixth grade. I'm not sure I can do it anymore," I confess.

"Just follow my lead," he says, drawing me out onto the dance floor. We fall in step with the other dancers and, although there are a few mishaps, I quickly pick up on the rhythm and the sequence of steps. I lose myself in the allemandes and the promenades entranced by how the twirling and spinning cause the women's skirts to furl and unfurl prettily. As we follow the caller's commands, we weave our way through the skirts that seem to have taken on a life of their own. I feel almost like a bee zig zagging its way through a flower garden.

After a couple of dances, we're tired and opt to sit the next one out. As I find seats for us along the wall, Jack goes to the refreshment table to get us some punch. I watch him, amused, as he balances two crystal cups on a crystal plate laden with cookies. He successfully reaches me without any *tragic* event. I'm so thirsty that I guzzle down the punch. It's tangy and has a sour kick to it. When it's empty, I hand it back to him, smile and say,

"Please?" He chuckles, downs his and takes both cups back to the punch bowl for refills.

When he returns, he hands me a full cup and says, "Here you go, My Lady." I take the cup and he sits next to me. This cup I drink slower. We watch the other dancers while we nibble on the cookies. My foot keeps time with the music, and I start itching to get out and dance some more. Jack sets the plate of cookies down and quickly chews then swallows the cookie he'd just stuffed into his mouth. He stands in front of me and holds his hand out for me to take. "Shall we dance?" he asks but just then the music switches to a waltz. I take his hand and allow him to pull me to the dance floor.

"I don't know how to waltz," I tell him.

"That's fine," he replies as he pulls me into his arms and leads me across the floor. I know I step on his feet multiple times, but he acts as if nothing has happened. Instead, he makes me feel as if we're gliding around the room. Everyone around us seems to fade away and it's only the two of us in the hall. A feeling comes over me as I look up into his face. I feel as if I can hardly breathe, and the only remedy is to hold him in my arms and kiss his face all over. That's the moment I realize...I'm in *love* with him!

Does he love me too? I wonder. The music stops and everyone applauds. The caller then announces that this will be the last number. It's not a group dance but not exactly a slow one either. We watch the other couples begin to dance, studying their steps and movements.

"I know this dance!" he declares. He pulls me into his arms and whirls me around the floor. Halfway around the floor I realize we're doing the polka! The man from the couple next to us lets out a loud *"WHOOP!"* as they prance past us. Jack and I crack up, laughing so hard we can hardly dance.

All too soon, the dance is over and it's time to go, but I don't want to. I link my arm in his and we stroll toward the door. The late afternoon sun shines through the open doors. As we step out into the street I'm blinded for a moment and shut my eyes. When I open them again, I'm on the couch in my house and Maggie is sitting cross-legged on the floor in front of me. She's staring at me with a half bewildered, half amused look on her face.

I inhale deeply and stretch. She's still staring at me. "What?" I ask, irritated.

"Whatever you were dreaming about must have been a lot of fun because you were twitching like you were dancing and laughing, and for a moment it looked like you were kissing someone," Maggie says. I feel a blush course up my face, and I cover it with my hands. "Oh," she adds, "and who's Jack?"

I groan into my hands and turn away from her, but she's persistent and says, "Ok, dish. From your reaction I'd say it's pretty juicy."

"It's nothing," I say, trying to make my face look disinterested.

"You've got a secret. Come on, out with it."

I bite my lip, shake my head, and say, "Nuh, uh."

"Don't make me use my powerful powers of persuasion," she says, wiggling her fingers, which is what she always does when she's about to pounce on me and tickle me until I give her whatever it is she wants.

I give her a withering look, but she ignores it completely. She goes to attack my sides, until I remind her, she'd pop my stitches if she were to try it. She sits back disappointed and gives me the saddest puppy dog face I've ever seen. "All right! All right!" I laugh. "I'll tell you."

"Good," she says, planting herself on the floor directly in front of me. She stares at me expectantly.

"Well, it's kind of embarrassing. You're probably going to think I'm crazy. Oh, and you can't tell a soul." Once she's linked her pinky with mine in a pinky swear which is the most binding of all promises, I start to tell her about Jack.

"Uhh, I've been having these dreams," I begin.

"And...?"

"And I always dream about this guy named Jack."

"Is he cute?" I can't help blushing and a grin stretches from ear to ear. "Your face says it all. Oooh girl, tell me everything."

"Maggie, they're just dreams. He's not real," I say.

"So," Maggie replies with a shrug of her shoulders, "it's kind of like reading a good book. Come on. Tell me all the juicy details."

"Alright," I say, reluctantly. I then tell her of how the dreams began and how I met Jack – of the concert, the picture, the carnival, and the dance – all the details of my dreams.

"Wow!" Maggie exclaims when I finish. "You sure have some imagination. No wonder you sleep so much. If I had dreams like yours, I'd be watching the clock till I could go back to bed."

I chuckle, realizing I *do* look forward to going to sleep – always with the hope of dreaming of Jack.

Just then we hear a car pull into the driveway. We look at each other excitedly. Mom doesn't come into the house for a while, so we kneel on the living room couch and peek through the blinds of the front window. She and Dr. Hunky stay in his car talking and laughing for a long time. That's a good sign. When he gets out of the car, we quickly lay down on the couch hoping we haven't been spotted. We stay there until we feel it's safe to sit up again and return to spying on them. He's helped Mom out of the car.

"He's such a gentleman," Maggie says with a sigh. We watch as he walks her to the front door. They talk for a long time. Or, for what seems like a long time for us Peeping Toms. We're on pins and needles waiting for him to kiss her goodnight. Finally, he leans close to her. We hold our breath, but then he kisses her on the cheek. We blow out our breath in disappointment.

"I'm going back and watching TV. I'm more likely to see a good mushy kiss there than on our front doorstep," Maggie says. I follow her to the family room, and we watch TV until we hear Mom come into the house. When she comes into the family room we turn around and look at her expectantly.

"Well, how did it go?" I ask.

Mom grins and says, "Very well. Scott took me to McKinzey's for dinner."

"Oooh, fancy," Maggie says.

"Then we went to an art gallery where his cousin has paintings on display."

"Oooh, super fancy," Maggie interjects.

"Then he brought me home and I'm here now."

"He brought you home like forty-five minutes ago! What have you been doing since you pulled into the driveway?" Maggie badgers.

"That's for me to know and you *not* to find out," Mom says and turns to go to her room.

"He could have at least kissed you goodnight before he left," Maggie says.

"Maggie?" Mom and I both screech.

"How do *you* know he didn't kiss me?" Mom asks.

"Oh, he kissed you – on the cheek," Maggie says, sounding totally disgusted with Dr. Hunky.

"Magnolia May Cooper! Were you spying on us?" Mom asks, her hands on her hips. Gone is the sexy mom who left this evening with Dr. Hunky and back is the mother who raised us.

"I wasn't the only one. Jenn was right there next to me," Maggie says with an all too familiar whine in her voice.

"Maggie…" I hiss, giving her a jab with my elbow.

She just looks at me and says, "Well, you were. I'm not going down for this by myself."

"I don't know what I'm going to do with you two," Mom says with an exasperated shake of her head. "I'm going to bed now," she says and walks to her room. The two of us sit there feeling guilty.

Then Mom comes back into the family room and says, "By the way, we knew you were watching. That's why he kissed me on the cheek. After you left, Scott gave me his *real* goodnight kiss." And there she is again, that sexy lady who had left for the evening on her first date in many, many years. Maggie and I dance around her cheering until we're exhausted.

Chapter 8 Hair

I don't think of myself as a vain person, but the thought of losing my hair really freaks me out. Gratefully, my hair is still intact after my second round of chemo. Chemo has taken so much from me already. My body is looking gaunter than it already did, and my skin is starting to take on a sallow look. I hate it. I feel ugly and I don't want anyone to see me this way, especially Jack. I don't know why I even worry about it. He's not even real. I still haven't cut my hair short yet and probably won't, considering before long I won't even have hair to cut.

I lie on the couch watching yet another movie. I'm getting tired of movies, but I don't have much energy to do anything else. My head starts to itch, and I reach up and scratch. When I pull my hand away from my scalp it's full of hair. Horrified, I scream which brings Mom scurrying from the laundry room. "What! What is it?!" she asks on the verge of panic. I hold out my hand with the clump of hair in it and begin to sob.

"I hate this, Mom! I hate this!" I cry. Mom sits next to me and holds me, rocking me back and forth while I cry.

"I'll call my beautician and see if she can get you in today for a haircut," Mom says when my sobs slow down. I nod in agreement and Mom goes to get her phone. While she calls, I sit on the couch with my hair in my lap, playing with it.

"I'm going to miss you, hair," I mutter to the lock in my lap.

I probably should throw it away, I think but I just don't have the heart to. I go to the kitchen and put it in a Ziplock baggie.

"Gigi has a cancellation for this afternoon. We have an appointment in an hour," Mom reports. I try not to touch my head while I wait but it's hard not to. I end up pacing the room and singing at the top of my lungs. Mom looks at me concerned so I say, "I'm trying not to touch my hair." She smiles and nods her understanding. The forty-five minutes before it's time to leave feels like an eternity. Finally, we leave. After a short drive, we pull up in front of the salon and park. When I get out of the car I look back and see that I've shed more hair and there's a big clump on the seat. I scoop it up as best I can and carry it as if it were the Crown Jewels into the salon.

"Come here, Sweetheart," Gigi says as she twirls her chair around for me to sit in. She throws the drape around me and secures it at the nape of my neck. As she pulls out the hair that's been trapped under the drape, even more hair falls out. "You know, Honey," Gigi says. "At the rate this is falling out it'd be best if we just buzz you. What do you think of that?" I look at Mom in the mirror and I know she's right, so I nod my consent.

I jump when I hear the click and buzz of the clippers as she turns them on. "Here we go," she says as she runs the clippers along my scalp. A torrent of tears race down my cheeks as my hair drops to the floor in a disorderly heap. Gigi notices me crying and hands me a box of tissues. She pats my shoulder and says, "It'll grow back, Honey. You know I just remembered. I heard about a company here in Portland who can take your hair and turn it into a wig for you. Would you like that?" I nod.

"Oh Gigi, that would be wonderful," Mom says.

"I'll tell you what, Honey, I'll just take this over to them tomorrow," Gigi says while scooping up my hair from the floor. She grabs a grocery store bag and puts the hair in it. I hold out the hair in the baggie and what I scooped up off the seat in the car to her. She holds open the grocery bag for me and I put it in. When she's all done, she spins me around so I can see myself in the mirror.

When I see my reflection, my hairless head, I'm filled with a mix of feelings all at once – horror, embarrassment, fear, relief.

Relief? Why do I feel relief? I think for a moment and realize that the thing that I'd been fearing the most has finally happened. I'm bald. I run my hand along my smooth pate as if admiring Gigi's work and burst out crying again. Everyone in the salon turns and looks at me. I know I should be embarrassed by all this attention, but I just don't care. Gigi removes the drape as I sob.

A woman from across the salon with beautiful, long, dark hair comes over to me and holds me tight for a moment and says, "It grows back. I promise. Look at my hair. It came back stronger and more beautiful than before my chemo."

My eyes widen and instinctively I reach out and touch her hair. "It is beautiful," I say.

"See," Gigi says, "everything is going to be alright." I nod.

The woman says, "I know how you're feeling right now. I bawled for a week when I lost my hair. My poor husband couldn't understand why I was so upset. But, of course, he'd been bald for years." We all laugh.

I stand and give the woman a hug and say, "Thank you."

"You're welcome, Honey," she says. Reaching into her purse, she pulls out a card with her contact information on it and hands it to me. "If you ever need to talk, just give me a call. I'd be happy to help you out."

"Thank you," I say between sniffles and give her another hug, then I turn to Gigi, thank her, and hug her too.

As my mom and I are walking out the door, Gigi yells, "Just remember, Sweetheart, bald is beautiful!"

I chuckle and say, "I'll remember," then repeat, "bald is beautiful." As I'm walking out the door, I realize I didn't bring anything to cover my head.

I think of turning back to ask for a towel or something, but instead I hold my head high and repeat over and over again in my mind, *Bald is beautiful. Bald is beautiful.* As a strong breeze blows past us, I'm struck by how much colder I feel now that my hair is gone. I pull my jacket up tight around my neck and climb into the car.

I'm grateful Mom decides to park in the garage today, so I don't have to display my beautiful baldness to the neighbors quite yet. I go to my room and cry until I start to drift off to sleep. Just as I'm about to, I have a terrible thought and my eyes fly open.

Will I be bald in my dreams? I think with alarm. I look at myself in the mirror and wonder what Jack will think if I'm bald. I know it's silly because I just see him in dreams, Jack's not real, but the dreams are such a solace to me, and I'd hate to carry my baldness into them. I don't want to have to worry about anything in them. I determine I'm going to stay awake and will not sleep. I go into the family room and try to read but my head begins to bob. I turn on the TV but that does nothing to keep me awake. I'm grateful when I hear Maggie's car pull into the garage. She'll be able to keep me awake. We can play a game. That should work.

Maggie comes into the room and looks at me, then does a double take and stares at me for a moment looking very confused, as if I look familiar but she can't quite place me.

"Jenn, you look so different! I almost didn't recognize you," she says. She doesn't come over and sit next to me like she normally would. Instead, she circumvents the room, putting her purse away, hanging up her jacket, looking at the newspaper on the table, which she never does, all the while stealing glances at me. I feel like an alien in some freaky menagerie.

"Maggie, just come over here and touch my head," I say.

Her face lights up and she says, "Really?! You don't mind me touching your head?" I shake my head and in seconds she's by my side caressing my baldness. "It's so smooth," she observes. "Do you think," she begins tentatively, "well, could I draw something on it?"

I snort with surprise. "You want to draw on my head?"

"Only with washable ink...nothing permanent."

"I'll have to think about it."

"Ok," Maggie says, looking satisfied for the moment.

Mom comes in with a scarf and a hand mirror. She gives me the hand mirror so I can watch as she skillfully wraps the scarf around my head. I have mixed feelings about it. I know she's trying to make this easier on me and the scarf is pretty. But having material against my scalp feels strange. I look in the mirror. She's done a great job and the wrap itself is attractive, it's just that on me it looks weird. I turn my head from side to side trying to convince myself it looks as good as if I had hair. Finally I say, "Thanks, Mom. It looks great." I smile and hand her the mirror because I can't stand looking at myself anymore.

She takes the mirror, seeming a little uncertain and says, "We can go shopping for head wraps after dinner if you want."

I cringe and say, "How about tomorrow. It's Saturday tomorrow, right? Let's do it tomorrow." If it weren't for my chemo appointments, I think I'd lose all track of time. Mom agrees and goes into the kitchen to make dinner.

I feel my phone vibrate. I pull it from my pocket and look at the text. It's from Hunter.

"Hey girl! How're you doing today?" it reads. I take the scarf off my head, put my phone in selfie mode and snap a picture.

I send him the picture with a message that says, "Lookin' fine tonight!"

He replies almost immediately with a picture of him just as bald as I am. The message with it reads, "Hey, now we're twins!" I gasp with shock, drawing Maggie's attention. I show her the picture.

"NOOOO!!" she moans. "Not his beautiful hair!"

I'm so moved by his gesture of support that I can't help crying. Mom looks at us with concern, so I show her the picture and the message. She gets all choked up too and says, "He's such a nice young man."

In unison Maggie and I say, "I know."

I text him back, "You're so awesome! That really made this rough day so much better. Thank you." He sends back a gif of Bashful when Snow White kisses him on the head.

After dinner I talk Maggie into playing a game with me. Mom decides to join us. "What do you want to play? Monopoly, Settlers of Catan?"

"Only if you want me to fall asleep," Maggie replies.

"Alright then. How about another game?" Mom asks.

"I want to play something fast paced to keep me awake," I say.

"Wackee Six it is then," Mom says, pulling the game from the cupboard.

Maggie gives me a questioning look. I just shrug my shoulders and pick which color deck of cards I want to play with. After a few rounds of Maggie winning nearly every round, Mom yawns and announces she's going to bed.

"It's still early, Mom. Please play a few more rounds with us," I plead. I know the real reason she's anxious to go to bed is so she can read in private the texts she just received from Dr. Hunky. She didn't tell us the texts were from him, but from the smile on her face I can tell. She relents and we play a couple more rounds.

After the last round, there's no amount of begging we can do to get her to stay. Maggie's ready to quit too. She goes over to the armchair by the fireplace, makes herself comfortable by draping one of her legs over the arm of the chair, and dives into sending messages on her phone. I watch for a minute as she reads a text and laughs. Then her thumbs fly across the small keyboard as she composes a reply.

I'm determined to stave off sleep as long as I possibly can and pull out a deck of cards to play Solitaire. After a few hands, Maggie says she's going to her room. Here I am, alone. It's quiet except for the ticking of the clock. I scroll through the music on my phone and pick a playlist I think will keep me jazzed enough to stay awake. I power through a few more hands, but it's a fight to stay awake.

I lay a card down, my eyes close and my head starts to fall toward my chest. When I realize I'm falling asleep, I jerk my head back up and play another card or two. This goes on for a while until I feel like I can't go on. I look at the clock and realize it's only been twenty minutes since Maggie went to bed. I stand up and do some exercises, but my limbs won't cooperate, so I sit down.

Maybe if I just rest my eyes for a few minutes I'll be able to stay awake, I think. So, I rest my head on the table in the middle of my deck of cards and close my eyes. I'm on our rock again.

"Da–!" I curse under my breath. *I should never have closed my eyes,* I think. Before I even dare to look to see if Jack is there, my hand flies to my head fearing I might find a slick, bald head instead of beautiful long hair. To my relief, my head is not hairless but full of the luxurious long locks I was hoping for.

"It's still there," I hear Jack say. I whip around to see him standing there.

Embarrassed, I pretend I don't know what he's talking about and ask, "What's still there?"

He grins and says, "Your hair and you're still as beautiful as always."

A blush threatens to creep up my face. Then he says the most unusual thing. "You should be proud of yourself."

"What?!" I say, thinking he's either crazy or talking about something else.

"You should be proud of yourself," he says again, and when I fix him with a confused stare, he explains. "Wasn't your biggest fear losing your hair?" I nod feeling rattled that he knows so much about me, but I remind myself that of course he knows this about me because he comes from my subconscious. "You faced your biggest fear and overcame it with tremendous dignity," he says.

I laugh and say, "There was nothing dignified about it. I bawled like a baby."

"There is nothing wrong with expressing your emotions. It can be quite traumatic to lose one's hair. And you, you stared it in the face and kept going." Suddenly, I feel quite proud of myself and decide right then that I was going to let Maggie draw on my head after all, because bald *is* beautiful.

"So sailor, what do you have planned for today?" I ask. This elicits a mischievous smile from him.

"Well," he says as he takes my hand and helps me down from our rock. "I've arranged for us to tour the lighthouse up the beach." He points to a squat tower about a mile away. It's white with three wide, red stripes encircling it, one at the bottom, one in the middle, and one at the top. On the very top is the light encased entirely in glass. It majestically towers over the craggy coastline. A sentinel and guide rolled into one.

When we arrive at the lighthouse we're greeted by several children of varying ages. They're playing some sort of game I'm not familiar with. Hungry for company, they excitedly cluster around us, chatting incessantly as we approach. My head swivels back and forth from child to child as they ask questions all at the same time. Jack turns to the oldest who's on the outskirts of the cluster of children and asks for their father.

"Oh, he's up there," he says pointing up to the top of the lighthouse. We look up and see the keeper, Joe Williams, sitting on a board suspended by ropes. He's busy refreshing the red paint on one of the stripes.

"Hello!" he calls down to us. "Children! Leave our guests alone!" he yells, then smiles and says, "I'll be right down!" The thought of being that high up with just a couple of ropes holding me makes me feel nauseous. I grab a hold of Jack's arm and look back to the ground. Without us noticing, one of the children has gone into the house to get their mother.

Mrs. Williams comes to the door and welcomes us warmly, inviting us into the house. As we walk through the door, the delicious smells of bread cooking greets us, making me salivate. The inside of the house is as round as the outside and there's a metal, spiral staircase on the far side of the room.

The house is spacious and is quaintly decorated. There's a large, oval, braided rug in front of the potbelly stove which is situated in the center of the room. A sofa and several wooden chairs, including a rocking chair are on the other side of the stove. Pictures of family members hang on the walls along with several still life paintings of flowers, fruits, and bottles. Next to the stairs there are paints, brushes and the subject of the next painting, a bowl of wax fruit, sitting across from a half-finished painting resting on an easel.

"Are you the artist?" I ask Mrs. Williams.

"Oh, no. I don't have time for that kind of thing. You saw my passel of kids out there. No, Joe's the artist. He loves to paint, which is strange to me." She shakes her head. "You'd think at the end of the day he'd be tired of painting, but no. He takes a lot of pleasure in creating his masterpieces," she says gesturing toward the paintings on the walls.

"Yeah," the boy who'd pointed Joe out to us says. "Being right on the ocean causes the paint to go bad so fast that something always needs painting." The boy talks much older than he looks, like a small adult. I study him out of the corner of my eye trying to figure out how old he might be. My study is interrupted by the entrance of Joe Williams. He wipes his hands on a cloth as he descends the stairs.

"Welcome!" he bellows. "I see you've met the Mrs."

"They were just admiring your artwork here," Mrs. Williams says.

"Yeah, I like to dabble with the paints when I've some free time," he modestly replies.

"You're very good," I say.

He nods his head in a bashful way. As I look around at his paintings, I recognize one. I can't place where I've seen it. It's of a ship tossed on the waves during a violent storm. The name of the ship stands out to me. It's called the Valiant Star.

"Are you ready for your tour?" Mr. Williams asks. Jack nods. Mrs. Williams goes to the kitchen as we begin our ascent up the stairs. As we make the first turn, we get a perfect view of the kitchen. It's quite elegant even by modern standards. The wood burning stove is flanked by cupboards both on the floor and on the walls. In the corner is a small table with a white and red checked tablecloth. In the middle is a vase with a few wildflowers, similar to the ones I saw growing outside. Most likely a gift of love from one of her children.

We spiral around a couple more times and come out on the second floor. This is where the bedrooms are. Each room we pass is neat and tidy with the beds made. Mrs. Williams with her passal of kids and no modern conveniences can manage several beds and keep her house neat and tidy. It makes me feel slothful because I can't even manage to make my own bed even once a week.

The third floor looks to be like a storage room. There's an area with a desk, lamp, and ledger. "This is my office," Mr. Williams says, "and of course the storage area." I see large closets—one is marked *kerosene*, another marked cleaning supplies. Mr. Williams sees me looking at the cabinet and says, "We need a lot of things to keep those windows clear. Everyday I'm up there wiping them down. There's this one flock of birds that seem to take great pleasure in taking a crap on them windows. Heaven forbid I don't get it cleaned by nightfall or there might be a shipwreck. That'd be my fault." The image of a flock of birds deliberately pooping on the window just to drive Joe crazy makes me want to laugh, but his look of horror at causing a shipwreck keeps me in check.

As we climb to the next floor, we pass a large window that looks out over the ocean. At first, I'm amazed by the thickness of the walls. The window well reveals them to be around five feet thick. I imagine that if I lived here, I would create a nice, comfy reading area in this window well. Then I notice the beauty of the ocean. It's a calm day and the sunlight glinting playfully off the undulating waves mesmerizes me. It looks as if there are diamonds floating on top of the water. Mr. Williams smiles and says, "The ocean on a day like today is beautiful, but on a stormy day, look out. You'd be grateful for these thick walls." He pats the walls in appreciation. "I'll tell ya, we've had to replace this window more than a couple of times. If someone were sittin' in this here windowsill when a storm hits, they'd be washed out to sea. When the ocean gets angry, she really takes it out on this lighthouse in a vicious way, but this old girl stands strong." With that, he turns and continues up the stairs.

We reach the top level where the light is. The lighting mechanism is huge and fills up most of the room. It's behind a thick layer of glass and there's an access door into the inner workings of the light to do maintenance. There's a man close to my age inside working on the light. Next to him is a large barrel of kerosine. He's filling a tank with the liquid. I look out at the ocean and see a walkway outside the glass encircled by a safety railing. "I'm glad that the railing is there. Don't you worry that one of your children might fall off?" I ask.

"Oh no," Mr. Williams says in all seriousness, "children are strictly forbidden from coming up here. It's in the regulations. Why I could lose my job if I were to let my children up here. They know they'd be tanned within an inch of their lives if they ever even try to come up here."

Not knowing what to say, I just nod my head and say, "I see." He takes us around and explains how the light works, which all goes over my head. In reality I don't even care. All I care about is the view. It's absolutely incredible. From the walkway you can see in every direction – a place to keep watch for ships sailing into and out from the shore. The ocean is dazzling, and I can even see Jack's ship anchored about a mile off. It's just a small dot bobbing up and down on the waves.

At the end of our tour, we begin descending the stairs. The smell of delicious food wafts up to greet us. When we reach the living room, Mrs. Williams steps from the kitchen and says, "You're just in time for lunch. The children have set up a table outside, and Joe, if you and our guests will gather up the chairs and take them outside, then we can get to eating."

"We'd be glad to help," Jack says as he grabs a wooden chair with a green seat cushion on it. I grab a chair that has a seat cushion that's brown with small, white, and yellow flowers on it. We carry the chairs out and sit at a table made from wood planks. A stump is holding up one end of the table and a wooden sawhorse is holding up the other. Our makeshift table is covered in two tablecloths that don't match. The table is laden with lots of delicious smelling foods. Steam wafts up off the roast, the mashed potatoes, and the bread, which appears to have just been removed from the oven.

My mouth starts to water and I'm about to dig into the food when Mr. Williams says, "Let us say grace." Everyone else grabs the hand of the person sitting next to them, so I take Jack's hand and the youngest daughter's hand who's sitting on the other side of me. She looks as though she might be three or four. Her dark hair is done in braids, and she's wearing a pink bonnet. Her hand feels warm and slightly sticky. I'm a little grossed out, but as Mr. Williams pronounces the prayer, I'm all ears. Maybe I'll learn more about how to pray.

"Our Father which art in Heaven," he begins. I like the sound of this and stash it away in my memory for when I pray next. "We thank thee for this great bounty we have before us and for our dear mother who prepared it."

Thanking God is a new idea to me. I'd never even thought of that. But it's not until the end of his prayer that he says something that digs into my mind and begins to take root. He says, "And help us to always look to the true light, our Savior Jesus Christ, and when we face the storms of life may we be as firm as this here lighthouse, that we might be a beacon to others lost in the storms of life." His words titillate my thoughts, but I store them away for later, when I can examine them more thoroughly, because right now this food smells so scrumptious.

As I'm eating Mrs. Williams' incredible huckleberry pie, I hear Maggie say, "Did you sleep out here all night?" I jolt awake and immediately feel the pain in my neck that comes from sleeping the entire night at the table on top of a pile of cards. I rub my neck and groggily look around. "Oh, that's attractive," she says laughing. At first, I can't figure out what she's talking about, then I notice a playing card stuck to the side of my head. I reach up and pull it off, bringing with it several more cards.

Great, just great, I think sarcastically. "Thanks a lot Maggie, you ruined my pie." Maggie looks at me confused. "I was in the middle of eating the best huckleberry pie I've ever eaten, and you had to go and ruin it by waking me up."

"Were you dreaming about Jack again?" she asks excitedly and plops down in the chair next to me. "Ok, Jenn, dish," she demands, then looks at her watch. "Better yet," she continues, "tell me tonight when I get home from work. I'm going to be late *again* if I don't leave now." Maggie gets up, grabs an apple from the fruit bowl, puts on her coat and heads out the door waving goodbye. Mom comes in just as the door closes behind her.

"Maggie's late for work again?" she asks.

"When is she not?" I say and wipe the drool from my bottom lip.

"Oh Honey, let me help with this," Mom says as she reaches over and pulls two more playing cards from my bare scalp.

"When do you want to go shopping for head coverings?" Mom asks.

I catch a whiff of myself and say, "How about in an hour. I really need a shower."

As I walk to my room, I realize this is going to be a new experience, showering without hair. I decide to look at the positives. First, it'll make getting ready so much faster because I won't have to do my hair, and second, we'll save on money because we won't have to buy hair products or pay the electricity cost to run the blow dryer, the curling iron, or the flat iron. This makes me feel better and I'm able to face my reflection this morning with a smile.

Chapter 9 Wigs and Hats

Mom and I pull up in front of a store that specializes in women's hair loss issues. A woman greets us and takes one look at my head and knows immediately what we're there for. She introduces us to one of their specialists, a woman named Ellie. I'm grateful for Ellie's expertise because I have no idea what I'm going to need or even what products will fill those needs. We start with the wigs. Ellie has us look at a wide variety of wigs in all different lengths, styles, and colors. The cheaper ones are the ones we can afford, but of course they look fake to me. I do see one that is close to my natural color, long and has a nice wave to it. Ellie has me try it on. When I see the price I refuse, but then Mom encourages me. "Mom, I don't want to because I'll probably like it and I know we can't afford it," I whisper to her.

She gives me a sweet smile and says, "Don't worry, Honey. If you like it, we'll make it work." Reluctantly, I try it on and look in the mirror. I look almost like I did before I lost my hair. "Oh Jenn," Mom exclaims, "you look so good. If you want it, I think you should get it." I want this wig so bad and for a moment I consider taking Mom up on the offer. But, as I look at the price, guilt takes hold of me. I don't want to cause any financial problems for Mom. She has struggled financially for so many years to take care of Maggie and me and I know that there will be more important medical costs coming up. I don't want to be any more of a burden on her than I already know I will be, so I take it off and put it back.

"I'll think about this one," I say. Next to the wigs are a type of wiglet or something. "What are those?" I ask Ellie.

"These are called Halos. She takes one down and puts it on my head. It's like part of a wig because it only has the bangs and the side hair. She goes over to a display of hats and brings one over and puts it on top of my head. With the hat over the Halo, you can't tell that there isn't any hair under the hat.

"This is genius!" I say. I look at the price of the hat and the price of the Halo combined and know I've found my new look. This combo is affordable enough that I can buy three different hats and two different Halo cuts – one short and one long. I've wondered for a long time what I'd look like blonde, so I buy a blonde Halo. I figure now is the time. Ellie tells me that if I don't like it, we can bring it back, no questions asked. I see this as a win-win situation.

Mom wants me to look at some of the scarves and turbans. I do it just to please her, but I have no interest in buying any. They just aren't my style. While Mom pays for my new look, Ellie's kind enough to cut the tags off the blonde Halo and light blue hat so I can wear them home. I look approvingly at my reflection.

"I look good blonde," I say.

"You do!" Mom replies excitedly.

We stop at the store on our way home. While Mom shops for groceries, I go to the craft section to find a set of washable markers. There are three kinds—the regular ones with all the colors of the rainbow, a glittery version, and a neon version. I think about what I want Maggie to draw on my head and choose the regular and the glittery markers. I also swing by the baby section and pick up a box of baby wipes and go to find Mom. She looks surprised at the items I put into the cart, looks at me and says, "I'm not even going to ask."

I smile and say, "Just a little sisterly fun."

"Uh oh! If Maggie's involved, it could turn into trouble," she says. We laugh because we both know Maggie and her sometimes not very good judgment.

When Maggie gets home later that day, I show off my new hair and hats. I show her the brown hair and green hat first.

"Looking good, Jenn!" Maggie says. "You really can't tell that you're bald under that hat. That is so cool." Then I go to my room and change into the blonde Halo. "Sexy," she says when she sees me. "Wow! You should have gone blonde long ago. You're gonna drive the men crazy."

"Maybe by being frightening. Because when they get a look under this hat, they're gonna go screaming for the hills," I reply.

"Jenn don't talk about yourself that way," Maggie says. I ignore her because in my heart I know I'm right. I walk to the table and reach into the bag from the grocery store. I pull out the markers and put them behind my back. I turn to Maggie and say, "I bought you something."

"You did? What is it?" she asks, sounding like she's ten years old. I pull out the markers and show them to her. She looks at me as if she has no idea why I bought her markers.

I pull off the hat and Halo and ask, "What are you going to draw?" She bursts out laughing in her magical, bird-like laugh – the one I love so much. I then pull out the baby wipes and hand them to her and say, "For mistakes." We learned long ago, when we were kids, that you can get most anything off with a baby wipe, especially markers. I sit in a chair. She studies my pate as if it were a blank canvas. She tries a few things, but half-way through she changes her mind and wipes it off.

After a few minutes of thought she declares, "I've got it!" I can feel her working but I can't tell what she's creating. It seems like a simple pattern with a lot of one color.

When she's done, she says, "Wait here!" She runs to the bathroom to get the hand mirror so I can see her handy work. I take one look and burst out laughing. She's taken her inspiration from the show *Avatar: The Last AirBender* and has drawn one big arrow from the back of my head to the front with the point coming down onto my forehead just like Aang, the main character. I pull out my phone and take pictures, and then Maggie puts on my hat and jumps into the pictures – the artist and her artwork. We have fun making duck lips and peace signs. We pretend to look cool and sexy, but we know we're far from ever reaching that goal. Still, it's fun and we have the pictures to prove it.

After dinner she wipes the arrow off and draws flowers. We take more pictures and I post them to my Instagram page, and title it Bald is Beautiful. I send some special ones to Hunter. I make sure I include those that have Maggie in them. I figure he'll especially want to see those. Maggie starts to say something, then stops herself.

"What?" I ask.

"Nothing," she says, getting up and walking to the kitchen. She peruses the contents of the refrigerator, moves a few items around then closes it, and moves on to the cupboards. When she comes up empty-handed, she sighs, rubs the back of her neck, smiles at me, and announces she's going to her room. I can't help but feel that something is bothering her. I grab the baby wipes and head to the bathroom. As I'm wiping her drawing off, I don't notice when Maggie pokes her head into the bathroom and mischievously says, "I'll draw something new tomorrow."

It startles me and I jump, nearly falling over. She puts her hand out to steady me and says, "Sorry, I didn't mean to scare you." I put my hand on my chest and catch my breath. She comes into the bathroom with me so we can talk privately. "I, I was just wondering if you're still dreaming about Jack?"

"Yes, why?" I ask.

"I just find it interesting. How are things going with you two?" I find her interest in my imaginary, dream romance a little strange, but try not to let it bother me. Besides, I do want to share with her some of the things that have been happening, especially the kiss.

"It's been going very well. The other night he kissed me for the first time," I tell her.

"Really!?" she squeals. "Tell me everything."

"Let's go to my room first and I'll tell you all about it," I say. I'm getting tired of standing, so we go into my room and flop on my bed, and I tell her all about the kiss and going to the lighthouse. I also tell her about Mr. Williams' prayer and that it had a profound impact on me. She lies back on the bed and stares up at the ceiling.

"Jenn, I have...I might have a boyfriend too," she says.

"Really?! That's great. Tell me about him. Is it someone I know?"

She looks uncomfortable again. She takes a deep breath and says, "I'm not ready to tell anyone about it yet, because I'm not sure how this relationship is going to go. But, as soon as I know I'll tell you about it."

"Fair enough," I say, and we lie on my bed and chat about everything under the sun until I'm too tired to keep my eyes open.

"I better let you go to bed so you can dream about Jack," Maggie says with a wink, gets up and leaves.

I get dressed for bed and slip under the covers. Light from the streetlamp outside casts shadows of the tree in our front yard onto my ceiling. The early summer leaves shiver in the wind, the branches swaying and dancing. I put in my earbuds and listen to music that fits the movement of the shadows. It lulls me to sleep. But I'm disappointed because I don't dream of Jack. I just have some dumb dream about going to the grocery store in my underwear. I know it's supposed to be a sign of feeling inadequate in real life, but I don't care because my dream wasn't of Jack. I wonder what a therapist would say about my dreams. They'd probably say it's a need to escape and they'd be right because when I'm awake I feel crappy, but in my dreams I feel healthy. Of course I want to escape from my reality.

I start the next round of chemo the following day. I'm beginning to lose track of which round this is. It could be my third. It could be the fourth. I don't know. The days have started to blend together, and if it weren't for Mom keeping track of my schedule, I would miss all sorts of appointments. I've heard that chemo messes with your brain. They call it chemo brain. I understand now what they were talking about. I feel like I'm walking around in a fog most of the time.

The nurse gets me all hooked up. Mom and I have both brought books to read. I try reading, but I can't seem to concentrate. I close the book, set it in my lap, and lie my head back to rest. It doesn't take long before I'm asleep.

Jack is waiting for me on our rock. I smile when I see him. He's so handsome and a lock of his hair has fallen out of the brim of his hat. I reach up and tuck it back in, then kiss him. "Where are we off to today?" I ask.

He winks at me and asks, "Would you like a tour of my ship?"

I look at the waves hesitantly and ask, "How will we get there?" He points to the rowboat he came ashore in. "I don't know. I haven't had very good experiences out on the ocean. Could we do something else instead?" I ask.

"Certainly," he says. "How about a rowboat jaunt around a pond?"

I smile and say, "That's more my speed."

He helps me down from our rock and offers me his arm. We take the stairs to the town where Jack hires a carriage from the livery stable. The horse pulling us is beautiful. It's coat shines in the sunlight. Jack helps me into the seat of the carriage, then sits next to me, takes the reins and we head to the pond. I rest my head on his shoulder and drink in the beautiful countryside. We turn down a road that is lined on both sides with trees. They've grown so that their leaves reach out and touch each other in the middle creating a tunnel above our heads. The trees have pink blossoms on them. The sunlight that plays through the blossoms gives the tunnel a rosy glow. I hear a squirrel chitter as it scampers up one of the trees. It knocks loose some of the petals and they flutter down on us. It's all so enchanting like something out of a movie.

At the end of the road are a cluster of houses. Children are playing outside. They wave and laugh as we pass by. On the far side of the houses, I see the pond. It's much larger than I expected. I would have called it a small lake. There's a boathouse and a dock on the shore. We pull up to the boathouse and Jack ties up the horse. He helps me down from the carriage and we walk to the boat house. In the dim light he finds us a rowboat and puts it into the water. He takes my hand and helps me into the boat. He then walks to the other end and gets in facing me. There are two oars fixed into brackets, so they can't fall into the water. He takes charge of the rowing and deftly rows us out onto the pond.

"So what's your favorite song?" I ask.

Jack gets to his feet, causing the boat to tip and sway a bit. He puts one foot on the seat, holds the lapel of his jacket and belts out a song I haven't heard before. "Oh promise me that someday you and I, will take our love together to some sky, where we can be alone and faith renew, and find the hollows where those flowers grew, those first sweet violets of early spring, which come in whispers, thrill us both, and sing of love unspeakable that is to be," he sings. I think he's done but then he continues singing, "Oh promise me, oh promise me. Oh promise me that you will take my hand." With that line he reaches for my hand. I place it in his and he unexpectedly pulls me to my feet.

"Uh, Jack...we're going to tip the boat over," I warn, but he just keeps on singing.

"The most unworthy in this lonely land, and let me sit beside you, in your eyes, seeing the vision of our paradise," he sings and pulls me close.

"Jack!" I scream as the boat tips too far and we both fall into the water. I gasp for air as my head breaks the surface of the water. When Jack's head pops up, he spits water out of his mouth.

"Well, that didn't go as planned," he says.

"You mean there was a plan for all that craziness?" I ask laughing. Although the water is up to his neck, the pond is shallow enough for him to stand. I'm not tall enough to touch the bottom so I tread water to keep my head above it, but the dress is bulky and heavy making it difficult to stay up. I manage to swim to Jack and hang on to him as he walks toward the shore. When the water is shallow enough for me to stand, I let go of him and walk the rest of the way. I immediately miss his warmth and start shivering as we emerge from the water. He turns the boat over and returns it to the boat house. We find a sunny place on the grass where we sit to dry. The shivers take hold of me, and I can't stop shaking. I feel someone lay a blanket on me and I open my eyes. It's the nurse. She's taking my temperature.

"You've got a fever," she says. "Let me go consult with the doctor." She's gone for some time. I just pull the blanket up around my neck and shake. Mom rubs my arms trying to help me get warm.

The nurse returns and reports, "The doctor wants me to give you this antibiotic." She injects it into the tubing hooked up to my PICC line. The antibiotic joins with the other fluids flowing into my body. I'm having a hard time staying awake.

"It's ok, Honey. Go ahead and sleep." I gratefully do, but don't dream of Jack. It's a restless sleep and before I know it, it's time to go home. The doctor prescribed an antibiotic to pick up at the pharmacy. Mom doesn't want to leave me alone, so we go home and wait for Maggie to get home from work. As soon as she does, Mom goes to the pharmacy to pick up my medication. I can tell she's worried. I don't blame her. This whole cancer stuff is pretty complicated and tricky. To kill the cancer, you have to be pumped full of poison. But the poison has all sorts of side effects that vary from making you miserable to killing you. I realize losing my hair wasn't as bad as some of the other things that are happening and can happen to me.

I lie on the couch and drift in and out of sleep. Jack's image flits in and out of my mind, but never stays. Mom returns with the antibiotic, and I take a dose. As Mom fixes dinner, I drift into a deep sleep. Jack is there, but we're not on our rock. We're in a cabin. I'm lying on a bed with quilts pulled clear up to my neck and I'm sick. I can't quite tell what I'm sick with. All I know is that I feel miserable. Jack is placing wood on the fire, across the room. We must be near the ocean because I can hear the waves crashing on the shore. Sparks fly up from the fire and silently float up the chimney. I try to speak but my throat is sore, and I have to put some force behind my words to be heard. "Jack," I say. I'm surprised that it came out sounding meek and timid instead of as a yell. He turns and smiles at me. He comes to my side and feels my forehead.

"Your fever hasn't broken yet. Would you like something to drink?" he asks. I nod. He immediately goes and gets some water from a bucket. I sit up and drink it. The water is cool and feels good on my throat. I can feel that my nightgown is sticky with sweat, and I get a good whiff of myself. I wish I could shower. As I move my head, I can feel my hair is mussed up into what feels like a fin on top of my head. It flops over.

Oh great, I think, *I must be quite a sight.* I reach up to flatten my hair, but it doesn't do much good.

"Would you like me to brush your hair?" he asks.

I want to say no because I'm sure it hasn't been washed for days and is greasy, but then I decide to let him do it. He goes to a vanity and picks up a silver brush and mirror. He hands me the mirror so I can give him directions, but he doesn't need any. He skillfully brushes my hair into some semblance of orderliness. As I suspected, my hair is definitely in need of a good washing. "I hate for you to see me like this," I say.

"Like what? Like someone I love?" he says.

"Like something that crawled out from under a rock," I say. "I don't know how you could ever love me looking and smelling like I need a bath," I say.

"Jenn," he says, taking my hands. "I love you no matter what you look like or how you feel. You are part of me, part of my heart. I will always be here for you, no matter what." He kisses my knuckles and says, "Now lie back and rest." My heart is pounding in my chest, and I wish for the first time that he was real. I lie down and fall asleep.

I hear someone talking. I open my eyes and I'm in my family room, but Jack is there too. He's standing next to Mom and I'm so happy that my wish has come true. I reach out to take his hand, but as I do his image fades away. It's my mother who takes my hand. My poor brain and heart can't take this. I squeeze my eyes shut and shake my head, groaning. Just then I hear a man's voice. My eyes fly open hoping it's Jack I hear, but the sound isn't quite right. I look around and see Dr. Pearson. He's comforting my mom.

"Give the antibiotics a day or two to kill the infection. The fever should come down by tomorrow. In the meantime, keep putting those cold compresses on her," he says. So that's why I feel all clammy. I reach up to my head and find a washcloth that has slid down the side of my head and is warm. Maggie comes with a new, cool one and places it on my head. It feels like ice compared to my feverish brow. It sends chills down my spine. I shiver and pull the blanket up around my neck. Dr. Pearson and Mom go into the living room and talk. Maggie settles on the couch at my feet. It's comforting.

"Did you see him?" I ask Maggie.

"See who?" Maggie asks.

"Jack. When I woke up, he was standing next to Mom," I explain.

"I didn't see anyone but Mom and Dr. Hunky. It's probably your fever talking," Maggie says.

I think about it for a few minutes and nod my head. "You're probably right," I say. I see something furry sitting on the table. "Did Mom get a dog?" I ask.

Maggie looks confused, but then follows my gaze and starts to laugh.

"Stop laughing," I weakly demand. She goes over to the table, picks up the object and brings it to me. I hold it in my hands for a moment then realize what it is. "It's my hair," I say weakly.

"Yes, and it looks really good on me," she says.

"You tried it on?"

"I couldn't resist. I mean how many times do you get to wear your sister's hair?"

I try to laugh but it sounds more like a cough. "How did it get here?" I ask.

"Gigi called Mom while she was at the pharmacy. So, she went and picked it up on her way home," Maggie explains.

"Oh, that's nice," I say as sleep starts to envelop me. I wrap my arms around the wig and pull it in close as I drift off.

Chapter 10 Remission

It feels like it's been years since I had the fever, but when I look at the calendar, I see it's only been a few months. The doctor tells me that this is my last round of chemo. I'll believe him because I don't even know what day it is. I had no idea that chemo brain would take such a toll on me. I'm grateful I'm almost done. If it weren't for my dreams of Jack, I would never have made it through this. Lately, all I want to do is sleep because my dreams are the only place I feel healthy. If I could get away with it, I would sleep all day and night. But Mom makes me wake up to eat, bathe, and brush my teeth. There are some days I don't even bother getting dressed.

But today is one of those days when I have to get up and actually shower so that I can have more poison pumped through my veins. *Yippee.* I plan on napping while I'm at the infusion center so I can dream of Jack. His kisses make everything worthwhile.

Walking into the infusion center causes me to automatically feel nauseous. I can't think of what it's called – psychosomatic or something. This darn chemo brain. At least I hope that's all it is and that when this is over, I will be able to think more clearly.

The nurse gets me all hooked up, takes our lunch order – all I order is Jell-O and pudding. When she leaves, I snuggle into my recliner and pull the blanket up around my neck and start to doze off. I'm almost asleep when I hear someone screech. My eyes fly open, my heart pounding with panic. We all look around for the source of the noise and see a young mother shushing her little girl. The girl's blonde curly hair flies in every direction, creating a glowing halo effect around her cherubic, smiling face. Now, how could anyone be mad at that darling little girl? She looks to be around two. She tugs at her mother's scarf, nearly pulling it completely off her head, revealing the baldness she's trying to hide. Once the mother has her little one playing with a doll, she mouths an apology to everyone. A nurse brings the girl a juice box and a cookie. She talks with the mother and plays with the girl for a few minutes before she returns to her duties.

I hear the man next to me grumbling. I turn and look to see if he's talking to me. His scruffy gray hair and face makes him look as if he's approaching his eighties. When he sees he has my attention, he blurts out, "Why she gotta bring that kid here anyway?"

Annoyed at his insensitivity, I kindly say, "Maybe she couldn't find a sitter."

"She knows the schedule. These treatments don't come as any surprise. She shoulda been prepared," he growls.

Oh, now he's starting to really make me mad. "Maybe the sitter had to cancel at the last minute," I reply as politely as I can, biting back the distaste I have for the man's attitude.

"Maybe that deadbeat husband of hers should step up and watch the brat," he says.

"WOW, mister," I begin. I feel Mom put a hand on my shoulder in an attempt to calm me down.

But then I hear her say very calmly, "Sir, I lost my husband to cancer. When he would get treatments, they didn't allow children to come. The presence of our girls would have brought him great comfort and kept his mind off the horrible things that were happening to his body. Do you really want to deprive a fellow patient of the comfort of her daughter? If so, then perhaps you should ask the nurse to move you to another spot in the infusion center." The man just grumbles something unintelligible and rolls away from us. I look at Mom with amazement. She handled that with such class. But, not only that, she's also never shared that with me or Maggie before. The thought of my daddy being in the same situation as me, but alone and sad makes me cry. I vividly remember being that little girl and how much I loved him and still love him.

A long, lost memory sprouts in my mind of a day when I was a little older than that little girl. Dad had put up a swing set in our backyard. I thought we were so cool that we had our very own "park" in our backyard. Dad was pushing me on the swing. He was careful not to push me too high so I wouldn't fall. It was a good thing because I fell out anyway. Of course I cried, more because I was embarrassed and frustrated with myself than for being hurt. In fact, I really don't remember feeling pain. Dad held me and wiped my tears away.

When I'd calmed down, he asked me, "Are you ready to try it again, Tiger?" I loved it when he called me Tiger. It gave me such courage and confidence. I nodded and he helped me get back on the swing again. I don't remember anything else, but the memory of his arms around me, making me feel safe and loved, fills me with courage and confidence to face this cancer.

The rest of the week goes by quickly with the help of Jack. Some of my favorite activities are exploring up and down the coastline. Sometimes we walk to our destination, other times we go further with a horse and buggy. He takes me to another dance held in the same hall as the last dance. I love it when Jack holds me in his arms and leads me around the room. As the dance comes to a close, the wish that Jack were a real person burns in me. I'll hold onto that wish for now because the truth is too painful to bear. I love Jack so much that the thought of him disappearing into the ether when I'm recovered and possibly never seeing him again breaks my heart.

Exploring the coast with Jack gives me an idea. "Mom," I say. "Could we take a trip to the coast once I'm in remission – to celebrate?"

"That's a great idea. When the doctor gives us the ok, we'll go," Mom says. Throughout the month, as I recuperate from the effects of the chemo, we plan our trip. Maggie decides to go with us and makes the arrangements with her job. Together we plan where we want to go and which route to take. Mom makes sure the car is in good condition.

My appointments with the doctor are promising. He's pleased with my improving health. The reality of being able to take this trip soon gets me excited. My strength and appetite are slowly returning. My dreams of Jack are becoming fewer and further between, which saddens me, but at the same time helps me to focus on returning to real life. As the dreams start to fade, they feel more like a collection of my favorite movies on a shelf.

Six weeks after chemo finishes, I have an appointment with the doctor. Mom and I sit in the exam room anxiously waiting for Dr. Milward to come in. Finally, there's a knock on the door. I yell, "Come in." The door opens and Dr. Milward comes in, settling himself on the swiveling stool. He sets his computer on the counter, pulls out his stethoscope and listens to my heart, lungs, and abdomen. "Everything sounds like it's returning to normal.

All your scans have come back clean," he says with a smile. "It looks like you're in the clear."

"Does that mean she's in remission?" Mom asks.

Smiling, he nods his head and says, "Yes, she is in remission." Mom sighs with relief and I'm grinning full throttle.

"That is wonderful news, Dr. Milward," Mom says, shaking his hand.

Just to be absolutely sure I ask, "Is it ok for me to go on a road trip?"

"I don't see why not, but…" he adds with an air of caution, "I want you here for another check-up in six more weeks. So, before you leave today, make sure you set up an appointment with Beth."

Mom thinks of another question, "When will her appetite return? She's still not eating much."

"It can take up to two months for it to return. Just make sure she's eating something. If she likes crackers, get her crackers. Let her eat anything that sounds good to her. Don't worry, her appetite will come back," Dr. Milward says.

"Thank you, Dr. Milward," we both say as he leaves the room. We gather our things, and as we check out at the front desk, we make my next appointment.

We get ice cream on the way home to celebrate, and I enjoy every bite of it. As we eat, I say to Mom, "Have you ever eaten citron ice cream?"

She looks at me funny. "What's citron?" she asks.

"I googled it once. It looks like a huge lemon and it's one of the citrus fruits that all other citrus fruits came from," I tell her.

"Really?" She pulls out her phone and googles it herself. As she reads about citron, I text Maggie and Hunter to tell them the good news. When Mom is finished reading about citron, she texts Scott.

When Maggie gets home, we put the final touches on our trip and start making room reservations. I'm getting excited about the trip. It's going to feel so freeing. I've been cooped up in this house for months. A getaway trip is what I need to help my soul to heal.

Chapter 11 Discovery

Our adventure is all that I'd been hoping for. Watching our house, and all of Portland disappear behind us as we drive away, fills me with such relief.

I'm leaving it all behind and the cancer is not coming with me, I think. *What if we never go back? We could move somewhere different that doesn't remind me of cancer and start all over again.* But, in my heart I know that will never happen. Then I think of Mom and how it must have been for her when Dad died. I realize how strong she is and hope that I can someday be as strong a woman as she is.

As we speed past the beauty of the coastline I'm filled with wonderment. I feel as if my soul is cleansed, leaving me feeling new and refreshed. I love it. We stop at several points of interest. Maggie's favorite is the Tillamook factory. We go on a tour and see how they make cheese, take "cheesy" pictures, and peruse the gift shop. Maggie buys a stuffed cow named Tilly. I buy some foods that look appetizing to me – yogurt mostly and some squeaky cheese. Of course, the *piece de resistance* of our visit to the Tillamook factory is a trip to the ice cream counter. A wide variety of flavors and colors cheerily greet us. The thought of eating some of the flavors makes my mouth water, whereas others make my stomach turn. I decide on a scoop of peach and one of cheesecake. Yum!

When we're done with our ice cream we go to the car. Maggie is driving this time. She gets a mischievous look on her face and announces she has a little surprise for us. We drive for about thirty minutes along the Tillamook River, around Pitcher Point and then we turn onto Bayshore Rd. which winds around and back tracks. As Bayshore Rd. draws closer to the coast it takes a sharp turn but instead Maggie turns right onto Cape Meares Lighthouse Dr. I can only suspect we're going to see the lighthouse. I have a mixture of feelings, excitement, fear, and something else, I'm not sure what.

Maggie parks the car. First, we take a short walk to see the Octopus Tree which has grown in a way that makes it look like an upside-down octopus. No one knows if it was a natural phenomenon or if somehow the Native Americans caused the tree to grow that way to use as a trail marker. Maggie, Mom, and I pose in the tree and have a stranger take our picture.

After admiring the tree we follow the path toward the lighthouse. The path is lined with trees which in places arc together to form a tunnel. It reminds me of mine and Jack's trip to the pond. We go aways along the path before we can see just the top of the lighthouse. We reach what seems like the end of the path and discover that we're at a viewpoint overlooking the lighthouse and the ocean beyond. We turn left, walk down the path a bit then turn right and walk the rest of the way to the lighthouse. It's a squat thing with a small building attached to it. The building had been used for storage and the two lighthouse keepers and their families had lived up the road. We take a tour of the lighthouse. It is only three stories high. The first level is used as an informational area with one lone chair. The second floor is where the turning mechanism is housed. When it was in use it had to be wound every couple of hours.

"No wonder there were two keepers," Maggie says. "It would be exhausting having to wind that thing every two hours all night long."

We then go to the third floor where the actual light is. The light had red and clear glass panels. The red and white light pattern was its signature. Each light had a unique light pattern or signature which helped mariners know where along the coast they were. Although this lighthouse was very different from the one in my dream it did make me think about Jack and the Williams family…and that huckleberry pie. Yum.

After our tour of the lighthouse, we drive on to Lincoln City for their biannual Kite Flying Festival. The city skies are filled with all sorts of sea creatures swooping, sailing, and soaring. It's magical. We sit on the hood of our car eating yogurt while watching the kites perform their sky dance.

After about an hour and a half Mom slides off the hood of the car and states she's getting hungry.

For dinner we stop at a cute restaurant that looks like a barn with a red silo attached. We walk in and are greeted by a young woman wearing a red and white checkered square-dancing dress. The knee length skirt has so many petticoats it flares out at least two feet. I watch her blonde hair, done in ponytails bob up and down on their coil like curls, as she leads us to the dining room that looks like a barnyard. She shows us to a picnic table covered with a red and white checkered tablecloth. It looks like it's made from the same material as the host's dress. The wait staff wear overalls, plaid shirts, bandanas, and cowboy boots. Animatronic farm animals sing, talk, and move along the walls. Half-way through dinner we're startled by a loud, "Yee Haw!" We look toward a small stage that looks like it's made out of wooden crates. Five young men and four women come out onto a platform and begin to sing and dance. One of the dancers is the woman who showed us to our table. Then one of the men starts calling dance moves and the couples begin to square dance. Immediately I'm taken back to the dances I went to with Jack. I want to jump up and join in the dancing, but I just have to settle for bouncing my leg to the beat.

After dinner, Maggie announces we'll be staying in Lincoln that night because she has something special planned to do that evening. We go to our hotel and check in. It's a room with two queen beds. We settle in and watch TV until Maggie tells us it's time to go. We climb into the car and head out. Maggie drives to a place with a big target painted on the side of the building.

"Where are we Maggie?" Mom asks.

Maggie smiles mischievously and says, "Just wait. It'll be totally worth it." Mom and I look at each other, shrug our shoulders and follow her into the building. Maggie approaches the desk and tells the woman we have an appointment.

"Welcome," Charlotte, the woman at the desk says. She gives us safety instructions, has us sign waivers that we know what we're doing is dangerous and we won't sue them if we get hurt. Once we've all signed the waivers, she comes around the check-in desk and says with a wave of her hand, "Follow me." We follow her down a hallway. "Have you ever thrown hatchets before?" she asks.

"No," Maggie answers for us. I don't say anything but have a few choice words for Maggie when we're in private. Charlotte leads us to a large room with lanes separated by chain link fencing. At the far end of each lane is a target. She hands us safety glasses and informs us that Chad will be over in a few minutes to teach us how to throw the hatchets.

Chad walks over as Charlotte is leaving. He's tall, muscular, and very attractive which Charlotte is very aware of. She looks at him dreamily as they pass each other. Chad though seems unaware of her admiration and just gives her a curt nod as they pass. He stares at Maggie for a moment then gets down to business. He demonstrates a couple of ways to hold and then throw the hatchet, his long dark beard wagging as he speaks. Then he gives us the chance to try. Standing close by us he corrects our stance, our arm position etc. When it's Maggie's turn, I notice he's standing much closer to her than he had with either Mom or me. He rests his hand on Maggie's lithe waist to help adjust her stance. When he corrects her arm position, he wraps both his arms around her and keeps them there throughout the throw and follow through. Mom frowns, moves closer to them, and clears her throat. Without looking he seems to get Mom's message and lets go of Maggie, backing away.

Good choice, I think.

Chad seems to hang around longer than he needs too. I can tell this is annoying Mom. She opens her mouth to say something to him when Maggie pipes up and says with her most charming smile,

"Thank you, Chad, but I think we've got it." Pointing to another group who've just arrived she says, "I think those people over there could use your help right now." He flashes her a dashing smile, nods, and leaves. Mom sighs while Maggie goes to her purse and pulls out a piece of paper. She unfolds it as she walks to the target and pins it to the target. When she steps away, we see in big letters the paper says CANCER.

Maggie turns to us and says, "I expect you to chop that sucker up."

I laugh, pick up an ax and say, "I'm going to enjoy this. Thanks Maggie." She's paid for unlimited throws so we each take our turn throwing the hatchet at cancer. It's a very satisfying feeling when I hit it right in the middle of the word. We whoop with delight, dancing around and hugging each other. Once we've had our fill of trying to destroy cancer, we go back to the motel feeling cleansed and happy. We sleep well that night.

The next day as we continue driving along the stunning coastline, everything I see reminds me of Jack.

I hope I dream of him tonight, I think. I hadn't dreamt of him this whole trip but he's always on my mind. We approach a small town and I see rocks jutting out into the ocean that look like the ones Jack and I would meet on, but these are smaller and more jagged.

"I'm starving," Maggie announces as we pull into the town. "Let's stop here for lunch." We agree and Mom stops the car at a sandwich shop. Something about this town feels familiar and as we walk into the restaurant I look around for some kind of clue. We order lunch and take it to the patio to eat.

"Where should we go next?" Maggie asks through a mouthful of sandwich. I look around to see what might appeal to me and see a museum a half block down the street. The sign says, "Nautical Museum". The teenage girl inside me giggles as I think of surprising Jack with newly gained knowledge of ships and sailing. I point to the museum and say, "Let's go there."

Maggie shoots me a knowing grin. Mom looks skeptically at the museum and says, "Are you sure? I've never thought you were that into nautical stuff."

"Oh, definitely, Mom. That place is a must," Maggie emphatically says.

As we walk into the museum, I feel as if I've been here before. It's driving me crazy. The building is old and has creaky wooden floors which are well worn and polished to a shine. We walk around trying to take in all the displays. There's one display of women's clothing from the late 1800's. It thrills me to see clothes just like the ones I wear in my dreams. I look down and see high button shoes like the ones I took off so I could feel the water on my feet. I try to memorize as much nautical information as I can until Maggie walks around the corner of a display and says, "Well, hello handsome."

I shake my head and chuckle thinking, *Leave it to Maggie to be attracted to some dead guy.*

I round the corner and find her standing in front of a display. A thick rope, the kind used on ships, cordons off the area. An old, tarnished sea trunk stands open with old clothes and a sundry of items displayed inside it. A ragged journal lies open in a clear plastic box, and the helm of a ship is fastened to the wall below a portrait of a sea captain. I look at the portrait and see…*Jack.* I stand transfixed and stare into the face of Jack, my Jack. The Jack from my dreams, the one that's supposed to be my imagination.

"He's real? How can this be?" I'm not sure if I think this or say it out loud but the shock of it all weakens me and I slump to the floor. Maggie, who'd wandered off to another display, sees me collapse and flies to my side.

"Jenn! What's wrong? What do you need?" I can't find the words, so I just sit and stare. "Mom!" Maggie calls, her voice near panic.

I hear Mom run to our location, but I can't stop staring. My mind is a jumble of thoughts and questions. Mom kneels in front of me, blocking my vision of the portrait. "Sweetheart, what's the matter?" she asks, trying to stay calm in spite of her mounting concern. The spell breaks when I can no longer see Jack's face and I look at Mom as if seeing her for the first time. "Talk to me, Honey. What's wrong?" she pleads.

Mom grabs my arms which releases my voice, "He's real, Mom. How can that be?"

Her concerns deepen. "What are you talking about?"

"Mom, tell me!" I implore. "How can he be real? He was just a dream, or…at least I thought he was. How can this be?"

She looks at me as if I've grown a second head, then looks at Maggie for a possible explanation. Maggie shrugs her shoulders and takes over the questioning. She rubs my arm and in a soothing voice says, "You want to tell us who you're talking about?"

I look around Mom at the portrait, point at Jack and say, "Him. How can he be a real person, Maggie?"

Maggie looks at the portrait and says, "Handsome, there?"

"Yes, Maggie! That's Jack…the one I've been dreaming about all these months!"

Maggie's eyes burst open. She points to him over her shoulder and whispers, "Him?" I nod my head in confirmation. "Dang, girl!" she exclaims. "You've got good taste."

"You're missing the point, Maggie. The whole time I thought he was a figment of my imagination! How can I have been dreaming of a real person I've never met?"

"Could one of you please tell me what's going on?" Mom asks looking from me to Maggie. Maggie holds up her hands, backs away and gives me a look which declares she's staying out of it.

I sigh and point to the portrait of Jack and say, "For some reason I've been dreaming about that guy for the last few months."

"Oh, but it's much more than that, Mom," Maggie interjects, definitely not staying out of it. "He's her boyfriend."

"Maggie!" I object, suddenly feeling how ludicrous this seems. I lie down on the floor, stare up at the ceiling and groan.

Mom sits down next to me to study Jack's portrait while Maggie gets up to look at the book in the box. "Wow!" Mom says. "He *is* very handsome."

Embarrassed about the whole thing I get up on wobbly legs and say, "I'm feeling better now. Let's go. I just want to leave."

With eyes glued to the book, Maggie holds up a finger and says, "I'll be there in a minute." Mom and I walk to the car to wait for Maggie. I'm grateful she's thoughtful enough not to prod me for more information but I can see the worry etched on her face. Then I realize why the building looks so familiar. It was the same place where Jack and I went to the concert and danced. I sit in the back seat of the car wanting to be alone and think. Ten minutes later Maggie comes out with something in a bag from the gift shop.

She buckles herself into the driver's seat, turns around to me and asks, "Shall we find a motel here in this town or do you want to drive on to our next destination?" Wanting to put as much distance between me and Jack, I tell her to keep driving, even though my body screams for rest. As Maggie drives through the town, I recognize more places where Jack and I have spent time together. The park, the photography shop, and the ice cream shop are all still there – with different tenants, different businesses, and different signs – but the buildings are all still there. It's all so surreal which fills me with an odd eerie feeling. I lie down on the seat and try to figure it all out.

As I watch the shadows of the beautiful scenery around us play on the ceiling of our car, my mind is in upheaval. I think of all the times I'd wished Jack were real and that we could be together. Now, I know that he was real, but I feel so conflicted and I'm not sure why.

How has all this been happening? I think. *This whole thing feels like something out of some quirky Romcom. Have I been time traveling?* I wonder. The thought makes me shiver. *Maybe I've just seen his picture somewhere like in a book or another museum?* I think, racking my brain trying to figure out where it could have been. When I can't come up with something concrete, I feel so desperate. Maybe it's all just that I'm going crazy. I feel it might just drive me insane trying to figure all this out. I decide to try not to think any more about it and shut my eyes. Moments later, they fly open again when I realize I might fall asleep and have to confront Jack. I have to figure all this out before I encounter him in my sleep again.

An hour later Maggie pulls into the parking lot of Depoe Bay Whale Watching Center, parks, and asks, "We're supposed to go whale watching here. Do you still want to do it?"

"Yes!" I say a little too enthusiastically. "Um, I mean I'm grateful for a distraction. I'm kinda going crazy about all this."

"Do you want to talk about it?" Mom asks.

I shake my head and say, "Not right now, later. Maybe when we get to the motel. I've been looking forward to this part of the trip and I don't want to miss it." We each open our doors, get out and walk into the center. There are many educational and informative displays about whales, their migration patterns, mating and feeding habits. You could become quite the expert on whales by studying the materials along the walls. A set of stairs in the middle of the room leads to an observation room.

I point up to the room and say, "Let's go up there." Mom and Maggie follow me up there.

As soon as we step foot into the room, we hear someone shout, "Look there's a whale!" We get to the window just in time to see it finish an arc in the air and land with a spectacular splash into the water. Moments later its massive body flies into the air again making an arc and turns almost onto its back before splashing into the ocean again. Before it is completely into the water it slaps its fin on the water's surface. It looks as if it was waving at us, and I can't help feeling as if it knows we're watching and it's showing off for us.

I hear Maggie giggle and say, "Why, that cheeky thing just waved at us!" We laugh with Maggie and decide to name the whale after our Great Uncle Lester who always had a smile and a wave for everyone he saw whether he knew them or not.

We watch the whales for another hour then decide to go to the motel. As soon as we're settled in, I start to pace. I feel so keyed up that I can't stand still. After a few minutes of Maggie and Mom watching me, I say, "I'm going for a walk." I leave the room as if I were fleeing a monster. I walk aimlessly until I find a park and I sit in a swing. I slowly swing back and forth as I ruminate on the whole Jack being real thing.

First, I realize I'm afraid. *Why am I afraid?* I ask myself. I think for a few minutes and then admit that dreaming about a dead guy feels so supernatural and it really freaks me out. *Why does it freak me out?* I wonder. As I strip everything away except the feeling, I realize I'm worried it may be a sign of mental illness, that I'm going crazy. I think about this and swing as hard as I can. I remember my prayer all those months ago and the feeling I got that it was a special gift from God. This makes me feel better, but there's something that's still bothering me. I isolate the feeling and I realize I'm angry, but at who? I twirl myself around in the chain that holds the swing and let myself go. I spin and spin in one direction then spin and spin in the other. When I finally come to a stop, I realize that part of me is angry with Jack for not telling me he was real. I feel manipulated and deceived. I grasp a hold of this anger and let it ground me, drive me.

I decide to go back to the motel. I look around and realize I've no idea where I am, and I don't even know what the name of the motel is. I check my pocket for my phone and am relieved to find it's still there. I call Mom and hear her relieved voice. Maggie tells me the address to the motel. Pulling up a map, I realize I'd walked nearly six miles. I tell them the route I'll be walking and before I can make it a mile, they pick me up. I'm grateful because the nervous energy that kept me walking earlier has now drained away and I feel exhausted.

That night I dream of Jack. We're on our rock. I turn on him vehemently and say, "I saw you in a museum today."

"I know," he says.

"When were you going to tell me you were a real person?"

"You…"

"You lied to me, Jack!"

"No, I didn't…."

"Well, it sure feels that way. What's that called when you withhold important information? A lie of omission?"

"You weren't…"

"Why didn't you tell me, Jack? It would have been nice to know I was dreaming about a dead guy!"

He stands there quietly with a sad look on his face. "Well, say something!" I demand.

"I would but you keep interrupting me," he softly says and gently takes my hands. Once I've calmed down enough to listen, he says, "You weren't ready to hear the truth." He looks me in the eyes and tries to pull me close, but I resist.

I shake my head and say, "I don't think we should do this anymore." He looks crestfallen and it breaks my heart, but I have to be strong. "Jack, I don't want to see you anymore. Please don't come to me in my dreams anymore."

I suddenly wake up and find I'm crying. Mom is awake and looking at me through the dim light. "Are you ok?" she asks. I shake my head, bury my face in my pillow and weep. I feel her hand on my back. She sits next to me on the bed. "Do you want to talk about it?"

"Yes," I whisper, my voice heavy with emotion. She climbs into the bed next to me and holds me while I talk and cry.

"I just broke up with Jack," I tell her.

"The man you've been dreaming of?"

"Yes, the *ghost* I'm in love with."

"If you're in love with him, why'd you break up with him?"

"I feel like he manipulated me and that my feelings for him might be based on a lie."

"Why do you feel that way?"

"Because he never told me he was a real person. He was just playing games with me."

"Did you tell him how you feel?"

"Yes."

"What did he say?"

"He said I wasn't ready to know, as if I was a child needing to be protected."

"What would you've thought if he'd told you from the very beginning?"

I quietly think but don't come up with any good answer. I shrug my shoulders and say, "I...don't know." The conversation dies with that, but I continue thinking about it throughout the next few days.

After discovering Jack in the museum, the rest of the trip feels silly and senseless. But I'd wanted this trip, so I try to forget about Jack and enjoy the rest of the trip. Even with all my efforts, Mom can see right through me. One night after a long day of sightseeing and hiking we go to our motel to get some rest. Maggie has already made herself comfortable and is lightly snoring.

Mom looks at me as I'm coming out of the bathroom and says, "You don't seem to be enjoying the trip anymore."

I shake my head and begin to cry again for the millionth time. She wraps me up in her arms and holds me.

"Do you just want to go home?" she asks. I nod.

Maggie sits up at this point and I think she's going to ask us to be quiet so she can sleep. Instead she says, "Yeah, I'd like to go home too." I chuckle softly and say wryly, "You can't keep anything private when we're all sleeping in the same room."

Chapter 12 Hunter Visits Again

It's a relief when we pull into our garage. It's strange, a short week and a half ago I couldn't wait to leave Portland. Sometimes there really is no place like home.

I haven't dreamt of Jack since the breakup. I'm glad, but I still have such a mix of feelings that I can't sort them out. I'm still in love with him, at least I think I am. Before I knew he was a real person I wished he were real. But now I know he's real. You'd think I'd be happy about that, but I just can't get past how betrayed I feel.

Shortly after we walk into the house, I get a text from Hunter. "How are you doing?" it says. Maybe it's time to concentrate on my flesh and blood boyfriend.

"I'm doing great! We just got back from our trip down the coast. I'm looking forward to seeing you," I write. Why did I write that? When am I going to see him next?

My phone vibrates a few minutes later. It's a text from him. It says, "That's awesome! I was just thinking about coming to visit you. Would this weekend work for you?"

This weekend? I panic, take a deep breath and dive in with a text back to him. "This weekend would be perfect," I write. "I'm excited to see you." I squeal and throw my phone across the room. Mom walks in just then and looks at me surprised.

"What was that about?" she asks.

"Hunter's coming to visit this weekend!"

"Oooh? That's good, right?" Mom says looking confused.

"I guess so… I'm not sure. I'm so confused," I reply.

"Well maybe spending time with him this weekend will help you figure things out," Mom says. She's so smart. I nod and go tell Maggie.

"Hunter's coming?!" Maggie screams with excitement. She bounces around the room like a super ball ricocheting off every hard surface it hits. I have no doubt her excitement is because she has a crush on him.

Then I worry, *If things work out between Hunter and me, it might just break her heart.*

As the time grows closer for Hunter's arrival Maggie perches on the couch in the living room, watching through the front window for his car to come into view. "What is taking him so long?" she complains.

"Maggie, he texted when he left his house in California," I remind her. She checks the time on her phone again. Once more she calculates when he should arrive. Then she checks my phone to see if he's texted, but nothing.

Finally, when I think Maggie is going totally berserk, she sees his car turn onto our street. You would have thought it was Christmas morning the way she reacts. She's at his car door before he can get it open. He rolls down his window and says something to her that I can't hear, but whatever it is it calms her down. I'm grateful because I don't think I can compete with her for his attention. I wait for him in the doorway. When he reaches me, we kiss, on the lips. It feels weird after kissing Jack. I reprimand myself for even comparing the two men. Actually, this is the first time we've kissed since I left college. I show him to the guest room and help him get comfortable. Our hair is starting to grow back. His is further along than mine. Mine is only about a quarter of an inch long, but his is at least a full inch now. I run my hand over his fuzzy scalp. He laughs and runs his hand over mine. It reminds me of why I was attracted to him in the beginning.

Maggie sadly keeps her distance. I can't stand seeing her pouting. I want to invite her along with us, but realize I need the space to figure out my feelings. Hunter and I go for a walk. We hold hands. Again, I think of Jack. This is going to take me a while to figure all this out.

"Now that you're in remission, what are your plans? Do you think you'll come back to school this fall?" Hunter asks.

I think for a minute as we stroll hand in hand. "I don't know. Being in remission is all so new to me I really haven't given it any thought."

"I hope you do. I'd love to see you come back."

"Maybe...I'll think about it."

That night as we sit around the table, I tell Mom and Maggie about Hunter's suggestion that I go back to school in the fall. "What do you think?" I ask Mom. Maggie gets excited and starts bouncing around in her chair.

"I think it's a great idea," she blurts. "We could be roommates!" Mom and I look at her surprised.

"Maggie, I thought you were going to go to beauty school here in Portland this fall?" Mom says.

"Well, I was, but something that Hunter said…" she stops and looks scared as if she's said something she shouldn't have. We all look at Hunter. He looks uncomfortable.

"Maggie texted me a while back about going to college this fall," he begins. "I told her about some of the great things she could look forward to if she went."

"I want to study chemistry," she declares. Shock doesn't even begin to describe the looks we give her. This seems so out of character for Maggie.

"How did you go from becoming a beautician to studying chemistry?" Mom asks.

She looks sheepish when she answers, "Well, Hunter helped me realize that the thing that I was most interested in about beauty school was mixing all the different chemicals to put on the hair and watching it change the hair the way people wanted. So, I took one of those aptitude tests and well...I scored highest in the chemistry section."

"Well," Mom begins, "you have always liked fiddling around in the kitchen to see what different ingredients would do when mixed together, but I never thought that would translate into studying chemistry. I just thought you were merely curious and enjoyed making messes."

"But, what about the math part? There's a lot of math in chemistry," I say, trying to bring the discussion back to reality.

"I've thought of that, and although math has never been a strong subject of mine, I'll be taking classes to help me learn to do math better," she says. Then adds, "Besides, Hunter's good at math. He said he'd help me."

Feeling a little betrayed, I look at Hunter. He's turning red and squirming in his seat. "How long have you two been texting each other about all this?" I ask.

Maggie answers hesitantly, "A few months."

Shocked, I stand up and shout, "A few months?!"

"Well, you and Mom weren't in any position to help me with the decision," she says defensively. "I needed someone to help me sort things out – someone who didn't already have preconceived ideas about me." I realize she's right; Mom and I hadn't been available to help her and she's also right that we both would have encouraged her to go to beauty school. Hunter was a good person to help her at that time. Shame forces me back into my seat.

"I'm sorry," I contritely say to Maggie.

She leans over and hugs me and says, "That's ok. I love you and I'm glad you can go back to school." With a cute little waggle of her eyebrows, she adds, "Want to be my roommate?"

Chuckling, I say, "*If* I decide to go back to school, I will definitely be your roommate." Maggie dances around happily.

As I lie in my bed that night, I think about the prospects of going back to college. It makes sense to go back to my old life, but in a way, it feels so odd. I'm different now so it wouldn't quite be the same. What if the cancer comes back? What then? And Mom, she'll be alone for the first time since she and Dad got married. Will she be alright without us? The questions dance circles around in my head. There are too many ifs that make it hard to decide. When I talked to Mom about it, she said she'll be fine being alone, but I'm doubtful. I feel so selfish wanting to go off to college and leave her by herself. All these thoughts are starting to make my head hurt. I slip out of bed and fall to my knees.

It's time to take this up with the Lord, I think. I pour everything that's cluttering my mind into a messy prayer to Him. Mentally, I visualize myself holding a package filled with all my worries and cares. It's flimsy and things seem to be trying to wiggle out, but it's tied with a beautiful pink bow which makes me smile. I visualize myself standing before God, handing it over to Him.

"I don't know what to do with all this," I pray. "I need your help knowing what to do." Suddenly, my mind is filled with images of me and Maggie going to college and being happy. I see Mom here at home busy and happy. I'm filled with the impression that God has accepted my package and is helping me. I also feel that these images are my answer. I should go to college, and everything will be alright. The peace I feel lulls me to sleep.

In the morning, I announce my decision to go back to school. To my surprise Mom actually seems happy. I thought she would be sad and worried, but she actually seems happy.

When I ask her about it, she says, "This is a new chapter of life for me. My whole life I've been Carl and Jan's daughter, Stan's sister, David's wife, and Maggie and Jenn's mother. Now I can be just me. I can reinvent myself, and I'm excited about it. Not only that, but I'll be also free to develop a better relationship with Scott." All my worry about her dissipates and I feel free to go back to school. Hunter just sits back and laughs as the three of us Cooper women dance around the kitchen.

The summer flies by as Maggie and I prepare to go to school together. I have to notify the college, apply for financial aid, register for classes – the list goes on. The most important thing to do is get the okay from my oncologist. He approves.

I'm grateful for all this busyness because it helps me not think about Jack. Since all our interactions were during his time period, there is little that reminds me of him. But every so often, a little tilt of someone's head or a phrase they use immediately brings him to mind and I want to cry. I can't help but miss him...terribly.

Chapter 13 College

Maggie and I settle into our dorm room and meet Hunter at the cafeteria. It feels so good to be back on campus. I love the whole learning process. I've signed up for all the same classes I had to drop out of a year ago and classes start the next day. I am excited for classes to start.

Mondays and Wednesdays I'm taking humanities and history. I walk into the humanities class just before it starts. It's held in a theater type assembly hall. The room is full of students and the only available seats are in the back. I take the first seat I can get and vow that from then on, I'll get to class early enough to get a seat up front. The professor stands and addresses the class. He goes over the syllabus and his grading system, emphasizing that he won't accept any late papers. He then talks about the assignments he gives and what the tests will be like. I am taking copious notes, not wanting to miss anything. At the end of class, he gives us our first assignment. He's posted the link to Vivaldi's *Four Seasons* in a link on his web page. We're to listen to each concerto and write a paragraph about how each piece makes us feel and what it makes us think about. The *Four Seasons* sound familiar but I can't place it.

I gather my books and go to my history class next – Modern American History. This teacher also goes over the syllabus, etc. Something on the list of assignments catches my attention. It simply says, "Fashion Show". Then I notice that this class covers the time period from the late 1800's to the present. I feel sick. I'd forgotten this class starts during the time period that Jack lived in. *PANIC!!*. My hands begin to shake.

I have to get out of this class. I can't talk about this time period, I think. Sweat beads up on my face and I start to breathe heavily. Then there's a tap on my shoulder. I turn and see the student next to me looking at me concerned.

"Are you alright?" she asks in a West African accent.

I don't know what to say or do. I think for a moment then say, "I just realized I'm in the wrong class."

"Which class are you supposed to be in?" she asks. "Maybe I can help you find it. I work in the registration office." Her gentle voice calms me, and I nod. After class we walk to the lounge area and sit on one of the couches.

"My name is Fatima and what is yours?" she begins.

"I'm Jennifer, but you can just call me Jenn," I say.

"So, Jenn, what class are you supposed to be in?" she asks.

"I'm not really sure," I tell her. "I know I'm supposed to take a history class, but I didn't realize this one started in the late 1800's. Maybe I'm supposed to be in the Early American History class instead."

She pulls up the class catalog on her phone and looks up all the history classes. "The time period for the Early American History class is from the mid 1600's to the late 1800's. Do you think that is the one you're supposed to be taking?" she asks.

The late 1800's again. I get all flustered and pull up the catalog on my phone so I can look at it as well. "It can't be," I mutter. "I can't study the 1800's at all. I... I..." And that's when the water works begin. I turn into a blubbering idiot. I feel her arm around me, trying to soothe me. I cry uncontrollably for a few minutes then start to calm down.

Once I'm calm enough to talk, she says, "Why don't you tell me why you can't study the 1800's and I'll see what I can do for you."

"You're going to think I'm insane," I say.

"I'm from Nigeria. I've seen some pretty crazy things. I don't think you'll be able to shock me," she says.

I chuckle, take a steadying breath, and plunge into an abbreviated version of the last year of my life. When I'm done, I look at her expecting her to be afraid of me or ready to call 911 for help with this crazy girl. But when I look at her, she's smiling.

"What a beautiful story. You have been given a wonderful gift from God. Perhaps by studying Jack's time period you may come to understand him better and come to terms with what has happened," she says.

I look at her with awe. "How'd you get to be so smart?" I say.

She smiles and shrugs her shoulders. "I don't know," she says. I decide to stay in the class. With Fatima by my side, I feel I can handle it. We exchange contact information and part ways.

When I get home, Hunter's there talking with Maggie. "There you are!" she exclaims when I walk in. "I was expecting you to be home a half hour ago. I was worried."

"Yes Mom," I say sarcastically. "I was talking with a classmate." I walk to Hunter and give him a peck on the cheek. It still feels weird to kiss him in any way. I put my hand on his shoulder and ask, "How long have you been waiting?"

"Not long, just a few minutes is all. Maggie was kind enough to entertain me while I waited for you."

"Thanks, Maggie," I say.

"Are you ready to go for that bike ride?" Hunter asks.

"Give me a few minutes to change clothes and then I'll be ready," I reply.

I go to the room I share with Maggie, slough off my backpack and change into shorts and a t-shirt. I go back to the lounge where Hunter and Maggie are waiting. I think for a moment about inviting Maggie but remind myself I'm trying to figure out if there's anything between Hunter and me that is worth pursuing. We ride our bikes across campus and along the river. It's beautiful. The path winds through lush trees and brush. Sunlight flickers cheerfully through the boughs of the trees and randomly speckles the ground with light. At times it seems almost like a strobe light or even a... a lighthouse. A lump forms in my throat and I swallow hard. I try not to think of Jack, but I can feel him so close. I'm so engrossed in my thoughts I don't notice that Hunter has stopped, and I run into the back of his bike.

"Oh! I'm so sorry! I wasn't paying attention. I hope I didn't wreck your bike," I apologize profusely.

Hunter grabs my elbow to get my attention. "Mag…" I look at him surprised. He gets flustered then adds, "Sorry about that. I mean Jenn, it's ok. It was just an accident. I was trying not to run over that frog," he says pointing to a small green frog calmly sitting on the side of the path. I wonder if Mr. or it could be Ms. Frog even realizes he or she almost caused an accident and lost its life in the process. Hunter nudges it with his foot trying to encourage it to move further off the road.

"Move along little frog," he says. How adorable is that? I love how much he values all life, even the creepy crawly ones. He recycles, doesn't litter, is conscious of the containers he uses, and reuses as many as he can. He eats clean, doesn't drink, smoke, or do drugs. He exercises religiously. He's even an Eagle Scout. He's more like a saint. I suddenly feel very unworthy of him. I wonder what even attracted him to me. I decide it's time to ask. We ride to the park and sit under a tree.

"Hunter," I begin, "what was it that first attracted you to me?"

He's quiet for a moment, then says, "Do you remember that dance where we met?"

"Yes, what about it?"

"Well, when my roommate asked you to dance, it was the first time I laid eyes on you. I watched you two danced and you looked like you were having the time of your life. You paid attention to him and made him feel good about himself. You didn't even know him, but you made him feel like a worthy human being. What you didn't know is that a few days before that dance he'd been contemplating suicide. That dance with you turned him around," Hunter says. "That's when I knew I had to get to know you better."

A warmness starts inside my stomach and spreads throughout my body warming my cheeks to a rosy glow. "You make me sound like a saint," I say.

"I wouldn't say a saint, more like an angel. And that's another thing, Jenn. You're so humble too," he says.

I don't know what to say, so I hug him and whisper, "Thank you."

There's a snow cone shack in the park so we ride our bikes to it. Hunter buys one for each of us and we sit at a picnic table to eat. Of course, it makes me think about Jack and eating the fairy floss. When I'm with Hunter all I can think about is Jack. Hunter is a great guy, but I just don't feel connected to him the way I feel toward Jack. I realize I'm not being fair to Hunter, and if my suspicions are correct, to Maggie either.

To test my theory I ask him, "So, what do you think about Maggie?"

At first, he looks afraid, then very cautiously he begins to talk. "Maggie is a lot of fun...and smart..." he trails off looking very uncomfortable.

"Well, what's something about her that you like?"

He looks really puzzled so I add, "And please be open and honest with me."

He begins to tell me things he's noticed about Maggie that I'd never really paid attention to and once he gets started, he goes on and on about how wonderful she is. Suddenly he stops, looking worried again.

I smile, put my hand on his shoulder and say, "Don't worry, Hunter. You're just confirming what I already believed."

"And what's that?"

"That you're in love with Maggie, and if my suspicions are correct, she's in love with you too," I say. He looks surprised but very pleased.

"Really? You think she's in love with me too?" he asks, looking very much like a puppy hoping for a treat.

"Yes, I do. I think she's loved you since she first saw your picture on my phone. Haven't you noticed how she looks at you, how she lights up when you walk in the room, and how she always has to be near you?" Hunter's smile broadens with each mention of how Maggie shows her love for him. Then his smile fades as if he's thought of something.

"But Jenn, I'm your boyfriend and I'm not going to turn my back on you."

I laugh and say, "You're such a Boy Scout, full of honor. Let me make it easier on you. Hunter, I'm officially breaking up with you. Now let's go get Maggie." We get back on our bikes and ride over to our dorm.

Maggie is sitting in the lounge trying in vain to pay attention to her textbook. When we lock up our bikes, her head pops up and sees us. We walk in and sit on either side of her. "Maggie, I have something important to tell you," I say.

She looks concerned. "What? What is it?"

"I have officially broken up with Hunter," I say.

Looking surprised she wheels around to look at me and says, "Why?! Why did you break up with him? He's like, practically perfect."

"Because he's in love with someone else."

"Wha – wait, what?" she says, trying to wrap her head around what I just said. She turns to him, and in all seriousness, she asks him, "You're in love with someone else?"

I laugh and say, "Maggie! It's you! He's in love with you!" The look on her face changes from confusion and concern to surprise and joy.

She turns back to me and happily asks, "He does? He loves me?!"

He turns her around, holds her hands and says, "Yes. Very much so. Being with you brings me so much joy. You have stolen my heart." He looks at the sweater she's wearing and adds, "And apparently also my sweater." Then he takes her in his arms, and they kiss. It's beginning to feel awkward, so I make myself scarce.

I go to our room to work on homework. I sit on my bed with my laptop and find the link to the music my professor assigned to us. I put in my earbuds and as I listen, a strange feeling comes over me as if I've heard this music a lifetime ago. I listen closely and realize with a shock that it's the music that was played at the concert Jack took me to. I yank the earbuds out and toss them on the bed. "WHY?" I scream. Wrapping my arms around my waist, I rock back and forth and groan.

Why am I constantly reminded of Jack? I think. *Maybe it's because everything reminds me of him. How am I going to write about this music? I can't say that it reminds me of my boyfriend who just happens to be a ghost. I have to turn something in.* I think for a while and decide to google it and see if there's something I can use. I pull my laptop into my lap and type in *Four Seasons.* This search only brings up hotels around the world. Next, I add the word music. That only gets me some old rock band by that name. Finally, I get smart and type in Vivaldi, the composer. *Bingo!* That search leads me to several websites that help me come up with some suitable answers for each season. When I'm done with the assignment, I feel drained and lie down. As I start to doze off, I half expect to dream of Jack since he's been so much in my thoughts lately. But I don't. He's a gentleman and he honors his promises.

The next day is the first day of math and dance. In math I don't see how anything in that class could remind me of Jack until I flip through the book, looking at the next few assignments. Of course, I'm wrong. In an upcoming chapter we have to figure out the height of a lighthouse. I shake my head. I just can't believe it. He's everywhere – at every turn. I doubt my ability to make it through this semester when I'm constantly thinking about him.

My next class is dance. I tentatively walk into the ballroom. There are students sitting on benches that line the front wall. Some are sitting on the floor talking to those on the benches. I walk to an open space on the bench and sit next to a girl with flaming red hair. She turns to me and extends her hand and says, "Hi, my name is Jill. If there aren't enough guys to go around, do you want to be partners?"

I smile, take her hand, and say, "Sure, I'll be your partner. I'm Jenn."

"Jill and Jenn," she says, tasting our names, "sounds great! We'll show these boogers how to dance." I laugh. I like Jill. The dance instructor and her partner come onto the floor. They demonstrate one of the dances we'll be learning this semester and of course, the instructor goes through the syllabus and class assignments. I look at the list of dances we'll be learning and roll my eyes. Of course we're doing the waltz, but what really flabbergasts me is that we're going to be square dancing as well.

Let me guess, I think. *They'll be the dances Jack and I danced to. God must really have a sense of humor.* Jill and I take the floor, dancing as if we'd been partners for years. She's really good and I can't figure out why she's in the beginner class. So, I ask.

Jill points to a guy across the hall with dark, wavy hair, a slender build, and a smile that could go on forever and says, "Because I'm going to marry that guy someday. His name is Nate." I stand there stunned. She says it with such certainty, as if it was a fact, but yet he doesn't seem to know she even exists. Then she adds, "Oh, he doesn't know it yet, but he will." That's when she whirls me around the floor toward him. We dance alongside him and his partner, but they still don't notice us. "Say my name real loud," Jill says.

I can't believe she's dragging me into this, but after she badgers me, I give in and practically scream her name. The guy with the wavy hair and his partner look over to see what the ruckus is, and Jill extends her hand to him and says, "Hi, I'm Jill. Can we be partners next class period?" Dumbfounded, he nods his consent. The whole while his partner is looking very put out. I'm shocked at Jill's brazenness and at being dumped already as her dance partner. Then she dances me away and says, "Ok, who do you want to dance with next class?" She looks around the room for a fitting partner. I have to put an end to this immediately or I might just wither with embarrassment.

I say the first thing that pops into my head. "I'm a lesbian," I say hoping that will cause her to give up on finding me a partner.

"Really?" she says with a smile and scans the room again for a suitable partner. "Ok, which one of these girls do you want to dance with?" Thankfully, the song ends, and class time is over. I sigh with relief, walk to the bench to collect my things, and head toward the door. Just as I reach it, I hear from across the room, "Goodbye, Jenn! We'll find you a worthy partner next time." I duck my head and rush out the door. I may have to drop this class.

Chapter 14 The Journal

To maintain my financial aid I need to keep a full load. So I keep my schedule the way it is. Jill becomes Nate's constant partner, and I pair up with the girl whom Jill ousted from being Nate's partner. I start seeing Nate and Jill everywhere I go and there appears to be a mutual attraction. Maybe Jill's prediction will actually come to pass?

Before long the semester takes on a routine. I go to class, something in the class reminds me of Jack, I want to drop the class, I decide not to, I go back to class, and the pattern starts all over again. I find myself thinking of him all the time.

I even see guys walking across campus who resemble him and for the briefest of moments I think it's him. Then the sadness sets in, because I know it could never be him. Whenever I long for him, I remember those feelings of betrayal.

Halfway into the semester we find out what the fashion show assignment is all about. The drama department has a bunch of costumes from the late 1800's and early 1900's. We meet in the Little Theater of the fine arts building. Our teacher leads us to a large room just off of the theater full of props and costumes. We're instructed to go through the designated costumes for the time period we're studying and find a costume to model. We're then supposed to write an essay about the advantages and disadvantages of the style of clothing. As I peruse the costumes, I have a hard time picking something out. It makes my stomach hurt just to look at the clothes. I'm beginning to think I'm going to have to take an F on the assignment, when out of the blue our professor holds out a dress to me just like the one I wore to the concert with Jack.

"I think this should fit you nicely," she says, handing it to me. At first, I'm frozen. I can't get my hand to reach forward to take it, but then Fatima nudges me and encourages me to take it, which I reluctantly do. "If you don't like this one, we can find you something else," the professor says.

"She'll take it," Fatima assures her. When the professor moves on, Fatima says, "That is such a beautiful blue. It's like the sky at midday. You will look beautiful in it." I nod and go to put it on. Just as I'm walking into the women's dressing room, one of my classmates walks out of the men's dressing room. I have to do a double take because he's wearing a dark blue captain's uniform just like Jack's. Although my classmate has cropped blonde hair, he carries himself with confidence just as Jack did... does. My classmate has a military air about him that reminds me so much of Jack and seeing that uniform on him brings Jack so sharply to my mind that I can't even breathe. I slump to the floor right there in the doorway and sob. I can hear and feel my female classmates impatiently trying to get past me, but I don't care. Some of the girls step awkwardly over me until Fatima comes to change into her costume. She sees what a mess I am and helps me to my feet.

"Come with me, Jenn. Let's find a quiet place to talk," she says and hands our costumes to the nearest girl who protests loudly. Fatima leads me to a solitary corner of the theater's lobby where there are several benches. We sit and she just holds me while I cry. She pats my back and says soothingly, "There, get it all out." Suddenly, a tissue slides into my view. I look up to see who's presenting it to me because it certainly isn't Fatima. It's our professor.

"The other students told me that 'the chick with the blue dress'," she says using finger quotation marks, "was having some sort of melt down. I followed the sounds of crying and found you." She looks down at me and says, "What's the problem? Was it the dress? You can choose a different one."

Fatima answers for me. "She's mourning her dead boyfriend," she simply says.

"Oh, well…um," the professor stumbles over her words, then thinks for a moment. "Why don't you go home now. Come see me tomorrow and we'll figure out an alternative assignment for you."

"Thank you," I squeak out.

She points at Fatima and says, "You better take her home and you can do a different assignment as well." Fatima nods her agreement and walks me out of the building. I tell her where I live, and she leads me to my dorm. When we reach the hall I live in, she leaves me trusting me to make it to my room by myself. When I get there, Maggie's doing an assignment while also texting Hunter.

Upon seeing my face and the condition I'm in, she jumps to her feet concerned. She grabs my arms, maneuvers me over to my bed, and cautiously asks, "Are you ok? Well, that is a dumb question," she mutters, "You're obviously not ok. What happened?" I fall down on my bed and bury my head in my pillow, Maggie rubs my back. "Should I call Mom?" she asks.

I lift my head and say, "No, I don't want to worry her."

"Well, then, talk to me," she says.

I roll over, look at her and say, "I can't do this anymore."

She looks at me puzzled and asks, "You can't do what?"

"I can't be without Jack anymore. Everywhere I turn there he is, or at least I think it's him, but it never is. Everything reminds me of him, and I just can't live without him...and that's the big million-dollar problem." I stop and stare out the window finally realizing the real reason I had to break things off with Jack. To truly be with him I might have to die and I'm not ready for that. Tears cascade down my cheeks and I bury my face in my hands. I feel Maggie get off the bed and hear her walk across the room. I'm afraid she's going to call Mom, but instead she pulls a book off the shelf above her desk.

Handing it to me, she says, "Here, I think you need to read this. I bought it at the museum where we saw Jack's portrait. It's a copy of his journal. They found it next to his decayed body on an abandoned island."

The thought of Jack having a body and dying shocks me. Every time I had been with Jack, he was alive or at least he seemed alive to me. Until I saw his portrait in that museum, he'd been a figment of my imagination, but this makes him that much more real. He had a body. He lived and he died.

I try to wrap my mind around it all, shaking my head in an attempt to get things to settle into place.

I take the book from her and run my hand over the cover. It's a midnight blue color with a gold ship embossed on the front. I open the book and flip through the first few pages until I get to a full-page picture of his portrait. Seeing it sends a jolt through me, bringing into focus how much I miss him and love him.

"Thanks, Maggie," I mutter, and sit for the next half hour staring at his picture. Maggie watches me for a bit, then turns back to her phone and her homework. I finally gather the courage to turn the page and start reading.

"Skip the first few chapters," Maggie instructs, "They're interesting and all but go straight to where I left the bookmark. That's where it gets really good." I find where she's put a square of toilet paper between the pages and begin to read:

"I am marooned. My crew and I had been sailing from the Solomon Islands heading toward the Hawaiian Islands when we encountered a devilish storm. At first, we thought to change course in an attempt to circumnavigate it, but our ship soon proved an inadequate match for the storm. We were quickly engulfed by the monstrous waves. The wind buffeted us as if we were a small toy caught in the paws of an angry cat. My crewmen fought valiantly to keep command of the ship, but it was all in vain. A massive wave tipped the ship onto its aft side. As it did, the mast snapped with a mighty crack, capsizing the ship and throwing us all into the ocean. When I finally breached the surface, I saw to my dismay that my ship was ablaze and sinking fast. I prayed for the safety and souls of my crewmen. Searching the billowing waters, I saw some of them afar off, floundering in the waves. I watched helplessly as giant waves pushed the burning ship high into the air then dropped it down on top of my crew, never to be seen again. In my despair I struggled to stay afloat. I searched desperately for something to hang on to, but just as I caught sight of a plank or barrel the wind and waves would carry it from my reach. I soon tired and believed for certain I was destined for a watery grave when something bumped my shoulder. As I looked about, I saw a plank, my salvation. I quickly latched hold of it, feeling for the first time that I just might survive this ordeal.

"The storm tossed me about for the better part of the night. After what must have been many hours, my strength was spent, and I felt I must let myself slip down into the depths to become food for the creatures of the sea. I prayed to God to save this unworthy servant from a watery grave. As I prayed, a beautiful woman appeared before me walking on the water. Whether she was corporeal, celestial, or a mere vision of a frenzied mind, I know not. She called me by name and said her name was Jennifer." I stop reading at this point and stare at the page with my name on it.

Could it truly have been me? I wonder. I look at Maggie who's been surreptitiously watching me as I read.

She notices me looking and asks, "What?"

"Maggie, could this really be me? I mean, he told me I'd been a part of his life for over 120 years," I say.

"Really?" she giggles with giddy excitement. She then jumps up, sits by me, and reads over my shoulder.

"Her white gown billowed in the blustering wind and tossed her chestnut curls about," the journal reads.

"That sounds like you," Maggie says.

"There are probably hundreds of women with chestnut colored, curly hair that he could be talking about," I say.

"But none that he loves and none that he visits in their dreams. It has to be you, Jenn. It can't be anyone else," Maggie insists.

I turn back to the book. "Her smile imbued me with peace and comfort. I watched her throughout the night, and as the sun began to rise, I felt land beneath my feet. It was a miracle! I had reached land and I was still alive.

"My body exhausted, I lie in the shallow waves on the plank which had been supporting me since the night before, or was it two nights ago? I had lost track of all time. I rested there until I could walk out of the water. Once I was firmly on the ground, I collapsed and slept. She stayed with me as I slept, coming to me in my dreams. While sleeping we explored the island together so that when I woke, I would know exactly where to find water and nourishment. As we wandered the island we talked. I shared my life with her, I spoke of Henry and his untimely demise, of my parent's emotional pain and the events that led to my leaving home. I held nothing back.

"What was surprising to me was that when I asked her about her life, she told me she had not yet lived on earth. So, instead we talked of her dreams and hopes for her future. She wants to do so much with her life. I admire her ability to imagine such a fulfilling future.

"After the second day of sleep, she told me it was time for me to wake up. I didn't want to. I feared I would not see her again if I rose, but she assured me that she would see me when I slept again. I felt satisfied and agreed to wake up.

"It was full daylight when I opened my eyes. Sand covered most of my body. Standing was difficult for the lack of food and water. I walked the width of the beach on wobbly legs only to collapse again at the tree line. At least now I had shade. As I rested, I attempted to brush as much sand from my clothing as I could. A stiff breeze blew away some of the sand and loosened a coconut which fell next to me. Being famished, I scrambled for a rock to break it open. Once open I admit manners were the least of my concerns and I drank greedily. Once the water was gone, I used the rock to scrape out the meat of the fruit. When all was consumed, I was quite satisfied and wished to sleep, but knew I could not if I were to survive. I needed to find water and food.

"I scouted the island discovering it to be exactly the way Jennifer and I had found it in my dreams. Fresh water bubbled up not twenty yards from where I had come ashore. I determined to build a shelter there. Jennifer had also led me to a grove of mangos which filled my hungry belly. The island was one of plenty, abundant with a variety of edible plants. I have also seen a large population of chickens and rabbits which have probably been left by seafarers for future consumption or even possibly survived a previous shipwreck.

"After finding the things that Jennifer had helped me discover in my dreams, I built a fire. It took some searching to find wood that was dry enough to burn. My search took me deep into the depths of the jungle. I found wood enough to last me several days near the mouth of a cave. I considered taking time to explore the cave, but when I looked at the location of the sun, I decided it would be best to explore it another day. I then determined to return to the beach but discovered that I'd lost my way. I could no longer see the beach and had made so many turns I was now hopelessly lost.

"I set the wood down and found a sharp rock with which I could mark trees. I then walked in the direction I thought I'd come but soon found myself right back by the cave. The next time I set out, I followed the markings up to a certain point then veered in an alternate direction, using a different symbol to mark the trees. I walked for what felt like hours, but still had not reached the beach. The sun was hanging low in the sky, and I feared I wouldn't reach the beach before the sun set. I plunged further through the jungle but still no success. A panic began to rise in my chest. I didn't know what to do, then I heard Jennifer's voice calling to me. I followed it for only a short time when I emerged from the jungle onto the beach exactly where I had started. Relief washed over me, and I fell to my knees and thanked God and Jennifer.

"The next morning, I followed the markings I'd made the day before and retrieved the wood and forged a more direct route to the beach. I started my fire, finding solace in the warmth of the flames even though the day was bright and hot. I stoked it as much as my fuel would allow, creating a grand bonfire. My hope was that a passing ship might see my flame and be alerted to my presence so that I might be rescued. Although I tended the flame as much as possible for many days, it was all for naught. While my fire burned, I set up a small camp near the spring that Jennifer helped me find. It was in the midst of a thick bower of trees. At night this tropical island can at times be rather chilly. As cozy as my little campsite is, I feel it will not be suitable long term. I remembered the cave I had stumbled upon and determined to go there on the morrow to investigate.

"That morning, before I journeyed to the cave, I went to check on my fire and look for ships. When I reached the beach, I saw that my fire was nearly out. I put more wood on it and scanned the horizon for ships, but there were none. I did however see that some things had washed up on the beach as I had. There were various pieces of broken wood, no doubt from the wreckage of my ship. I gathered them and placed them near my fire. Yet, there was something more. Something much larger. It toppled in the waves. I waded out to retrieve it and pulled it ashore. The waves were treacherous and nearly dragged me into the deep again. At last I was able to drag it safely aground. It was my trunk. I was most pleased to have this trunk again. It will prove most useful. I dragged it to my campsite and opened it. Inside were several items of clothing. It will feel refreshing to be able to put on clean clothes once they are washed. Amongst the clothing, there were another pair of boots, some candles, a cutlass, a Bible, and this journal which my mother gave me. Each item brought me joy to possess. I laid out the items to dry, went to my fire and made a torch. I then made my way to the cave.

"With the abundant moisture of the jungle, it was difficult to keep my torch lit. Water ran off leaves and threatened to extinguish the flame. I used the cutlass to slash away at the overgrowth of foliage. At last I arrived at my destination with my torch still lit. I entered the maw of the cave which was small and forced me to bend to enter. Once inside I was quite surprised by the spaciousness of the cave. The opening was very deceiving. What appeared to me to be a small, cozy cave was in reality as large as one of the plantation homes of the South.

"I endeavored to explore the cave. At first, I wound my way around the outskirts of the cavity attempting to avoid the stalactites and stalagmites. Unfortunately, the smaller ones close to the ground proved difficult to see and more than once I found myself toppling to the ground. As I circled back around to the front of the cave, I stumbled over what I believed to be yet another stalagmite, but as the light of the torch shone on the object I'd fallen over, I discovered it to be, in reality, human remains. I sat back and studied the corpse. The skeleton wore a three-cornered hat in the same fashion of the sea captains of the last century, and a captain's jacket. No doubt this gentleman was marooned here as well, but many years before. At first, I felt sorrow for the poor gentleman, but then I realized I too might join him in his fate. The thought fills me with despair."

I stop there in my reading to cry. The thought of Jack being in such a desperate situation and feeling such despair makes me hurt. I wish I could go back to that time and help him, then the thought hits me.

I was there. I was with him through this ordeal. The thought fills me with peace, and I return to my reading. There's a large gap in years between what I had just read and the next entry.

"Captain Pennyworth and I have been together on this island for five years now, by my calculations."

"Captain Pennyworth?" I ask, looking to Maggie for some answers. The name sounds familiar, but I can't place it.

She gives me a quizzical look then gasps, "Wasn't that what we named that skeleton in Dr. Milward's office?"

"That's right!" I say. I sit and feel the magnitude of the fact that I'd named our skeleton the same name that Jack had named his. Finally, I take a deep breath and turn back to the journal.

"It has been years since I've written in this journal. I chose not to write because life had become so mundane and dreary. My despair had gotten so severe I contemplated taking my own life, but my sweet Jennifer came to me in a dream and suggested I retrieve the bones from the cave to act as a companion. Although it's not the same as having a live person, keeping Captain Pennyworth around does stave off complete loneliness.

"Jennifer comes to me in my dreams only occasionally, usually when I'm feeling most desperate. The sight of her brings great comfort and..."

The narrative stops there for over a year. I can't help wondering what caused him to stop writing, but his next entry is quite grave.

"I have fallen. I had washed my ragged clothing in an attempt to smell good. In hindsight, it seems it was a ridiculous decision. I had laid the clothes on the bushes to dry. When it was nearly dry, a gust of wind carried my shirt up into a tree. I have climbed this particular tree hundreds of times over the years I have been on this island, so I had no concerns for my safety. Unfortunately, when I was almost to the shirt a branch gave way and I fell. On the way down, my leg became entangled in some vines and was broken in the fall. I passed out for a time, dangling there for...I don't know how long. When I awoke, the pain was excruciating, and I could see the bone protruding from the skin. I struggled for a time, and finally was able to free myself from the vines. I landed hard on the ground at the base of the tree. It was very painful and nearly lost consciousness, but with pure grit and determination I was able to stay awake.

I've made myself comfortable as best I can, but each time I move to retrieve something I need I'm filled anew with excruciating pain. I'm sure that if Captain Pennyworth was alive, he'd cover his ears from my screams of pain and frustration."

Several days go by before he writes again. His sentences are disjointed and don't make much sense. What is clear is that he's not doing well and is probably dying.

"...fever has set in...so cold...can't stop shivering...Jennifer is waiting for me on the beach...I can't get to her...I see her smile...I see her hand...out to me...must go..."

That's it. That's all he wrote. I wipe away the tears coursing down my cheeks and look at Maggie. She's crying too.

"I feel so bad for him," Maggie says. "That must have been a terrible way to die. The poor man, all alone."

"But he wasn't alone," I say. "I was there with him."

Maggie smiles and says, "Yes, you were." She points to the book and says, "The last chapter is how they found Jack and Captain Pennyworth during World War II." She takes the book from me, turns to the very end and shows me a photo taken more than a hundred years ago. It takes my breath away because it's the picture Jack and I had taken at the photo shop.

"How did this picture get in this book?" I ask her.

"So, it is you, isn't it?" Maggie says.

"Jack and I had it taken by a man in a photo shop in that town with the museum. But it was just a dream. How can it be in this book over a hundred years later?" My head starts to buzz with so many questions that don't appear to have any answers.

Maggie just shrugs her shoulders and says, "Miracles?"

I stare at the photo and run my hand along it trying to remember everything from that day. I look at the title of the picture. It says *Captain Jack Callahan with an unknown woman with the Mona Lisa Smile*. I stare at the picture and smile until exhaustion starts to creep through the corners of my mind and into my body. I press the open book with the picture of Jack and me, to my chest, lie down and fall asleep.

I'm not on our rock. This time I'm in the backyard of our home in Portland. My dad is here and he's pushing me on the swing.

"Hey Tiger, how're you doing?" he asks me.

I pump harder. "Not so good, Dad," I say. "Where's Jack?"

"Patience, Tiger," he says with a chuckle. "He'll be coming soon, but not today."

I keep swinging. I look up at the clear blue sky, hear the leaves rustling in the breeze, smell the freshly mown grass and feel the wind ruffle my hair. I feel like a child again – safe and secure in my own backyard with my daddy. He sits in the swing next to mine. I drag my feet until I come to a stop. Dad reaches over and takes my hand.

"You know, I'm proud of you," he says.

I smile and say, "You are? Why?"

"You've been such a comfort to your mother. You've watched over her and your sister. And you've always tried to be a good person."

"Thanks, Dad."

"Soon, things are going to get really rough for you, your mother, and Maggie. But I want you to always remember that Jack and I will be by your side the whole time. In fact, God has a lot of help planned for all my girls," he says. Until that moment I'd forgotten that he used to call us his girls. He gets up, kisses me on the cheek, pushes me one more time and disappears.

Chapter 15 Thanksgiving

The semester seems to go incredibly fast. Midterms are over and Thanksgiving is just around the corner. I'm looking forward to going home and seeing Mom. I want to tell her and Maggie about my dream of Dad, but I don't want them to worry.

As I get dressed for the day, I slide on my jeans and try to button them up. They're tight. My belly is bigger than it used to be.

I better not eat so much, I think. I opt for some leggings and a long t-shirt and go to class.

That evening, Hunter calls to see if he could come over and talk to me. It feels a little strange to be talking to him now that he's dating my sister. I meet him down in the lounge. The noise of some guys playing ping pong makes it hard to hear. He pulls me over to a quieter, semi-secluded area. "I want to show you something," he says and pulls a small box out of his coat pocket. He opens it and inside is a ring box. I'm confused. He then opens the hinged box and inside is a diamond ring.

What is he doing with a ring and why is he showing it to me? I wonder

"So help me, Hunter, if you get down on one knee and propose to me, I'm going to slug you!" I threaten.

"Wha...What?" he says, looking very confused. After a moment of thought he realizes what it must look like. "Oh," he says with a chuckle. "No, this is for Maggie. I'm going to propose to her tomorrow night. I just need to know if this is something she will like," he explains.

"Awwww," is my first response. Then I take a better look at the ring and say, "It's beautiful, Hunter. Yes, she will love it. To tell you the truth it could be a ring from a box of cereal and it wouldn't matter to her because it came from you." He grins, delighted with the news. "How're you going to pop the question?" I ask.

"I'm taking her to dinner at that fancy French restaurant across town, then for a walk through the park. When we get to the fountain, I'm going to get on one knee and confess my unswerving loyalty to her. Then I'm going to ask her to marry me," he says.

"She'll love it, Hunter. Good choice," I say.

"What's a good choice?" Maggie asks. Hunter hurries to put the box away. She's looking suspicious.

"He was just telling me he's thinking of changing gyms," I fib, grateful I could fabricate one so quickly. "He told me he was thinking about that gym next to the mall and I was just telling him it was a good choice." She looks skeptical but lets the subject rest.

The next night I help Maggie get ready for her date with Hunter. "Do you know where he's taking you tonight?" I ask.

"No, but he said to dress nice so I'm guessing it'll be fancy," she says as she adjusts her sheer, coral sleeves. She looks like a goddess as she moves across the room to retrieve her necklace and matching earrings. The tea length, chiffon skirt flounces playfully as she moves. The bodice is lace with a scoop neckline.

I can't help but be excited for her. Having Hunter as a brother-in-law feels more right than having him as a boyfriend ever did. In fact, it feels perfect. Maggie turns and looks as if she wants to tell me something. But her phone buzzes. Hunter is downstairs waiting for her. We ride the elevator together. When the doors open Hunter is waiting for her. He's wearing a black tuxedo and is carrying a corsage. It's starting to feel more like prom than a proposal. Hunter takes the corsage out of the box, slips it over her hand and onto her wrist. Maggie admires it for a moment, then gives Hunter a kiss on the cheek. A gentle blush inches across his face.

Oh, he's so gaga for her. It's so dang cute, I think.

They start to leave, but I stop them. Following in the tradition of proms, I decide I need to take a picture...for Mom. They pose by the planter at the front doors to our hall and I snap a picture or two...ok, three. After they leave, I send the pics to Mom.

As I walk toward the elevator, I catch my side reflection in a mirror. I'm shocked when I see how big my belly has gotten.

I don't understand, I think. *I've been watching what I eat for the last couple of days. How could I be getting bigger?* I decide to give it a few more days. *Maybe I'm just retaining water because of my cycle,* I think. All the same, I call Mom and ask her to make an appointment with my doctor during the week we'll be home for Thanksgiving. We leave in just a few days. Hopefully, it's nothing serious. I ride the elevator to our room and study for the quiz in Math tomorrow. I want to be awake when Maggie gets home, but I start to feel sleepy as I study, so I put my head down for just a few minutes.

I'm jolted awake by Maggie coming in the door. I raise my head and look at the clock. My few minutes snooze had turned into a two-hour nap. I groggily look at her. She's dripping wet and is wearing Hunter's tux coat. Her hair is plastered to her beaming face. She laughs when she sees my face and sticks her hand out to show me that the ring Hunter showed me yesterday is now gleaming on her finger. It's a perfect fit in more ways than one. We scream, laugh and dance around, hugging each other until the girl in the room next door pounds on the wall. We giggle and try to quiet down, but before long we're loud again. The neighbor girl pounds on the wall again. I yell, "Maggie just got engaged!"

"Good for her. Now can you quiet down?" is the girl's deadpan response. Maggie gives me another wet hug, which prompts me to ask why she's all wet.

"Let me change and I'll tell you every single detail," she says. She grabs dry clothes from her drawer and goes into the bathroom to change. While she's changing her clothes, I change out of my now wet pajamas and wait on my bed. A few moments later she comes out in her pajamas, towel drying her hair. She sits on my bed and folds her legs up underneath herself.

"Ok, tell me everything," I insist.

"Well, he took me to Jacque's, that French restaurant on Marsh Boulevard," she says with a twinkle in her eyes. "Have you ever been there?" I shake my head. "Well, it's super fancy. I tried escargot for the first time. I didn't like the texture, but the sauce was good. Thankfully, it was a sampler platter, or I'd be super hungry right now. Anyway, it was so romantic because this violinist came over and was playing for us like you see in the movies."

"Yeah, you never see that kind of thing at the restaurants we go to," I say.

She chuckles and says, "Could you imagine a violinist walking around Eddy's Burgers?"

"Forget Eddy's, tell me about tonight," I demand.

"Well, after dinner we went for a walk through the park and when we got to the fountain, he stopped me. He took my hands in his and told me how much he loves me and that he can't imagine living the rest of his life without me. I thought he was going to ask me to move in with him, but he's too much of a gentleman to do that. Then he gets down on one knee and pulls out a box with this ring in it!"

I have to shoosh her because in her excitement she's starting to get too loud for the neighbor girl.

"I screamed, of course and started jumping around and tripped and in true Maggie fashion, fell right into the fountain," she says. We laugh till our sides hurt.

"What did Hunter do?" I ask.

"Well, he helped me out and asked, 'So is that a, yes?' and I said, 'It is most definitely a yes'. That's when he slipped the ring on my finger, and we kissed." At this memory she sighs and looks dreamily off, lost in the memory of that moment. Then she holds her hand out in front of herself to admire the ring again or maybe to assure herself that it wasn't just a dream. It sparkles brilliantly in the light. I grow melancholy as I watch her, jealous that she'll have the happily-ever-after with the man she loves, that I can never have with the man I love. I try to stuff it down so I can be happy for Maggie in her special moment, but it makes my stomachache.

"You look tired. I should let you go to bed," she says. I'm grateful because I fear that this pain may be too hard to hide.

I give her a kiss on the cheek and say, "Thank you...I love you and am very happy for you."

She hugs me and says, "Thanks. That means a lot to me since he was your boyfriend first."

As we settle into our respective beds, I say what we've said to each other since we were little, "Good night. Sleep tight. Don't let the beddy bugs bite."

"I don't think I'm going to sleep much tonight. I've got a wedding to plan," she says but within a few minutes she's lightly snoring. I turn on the light on my phone, pull out Jack's journal, and look at the pictures of him and the one of us together until I fall asleep. When I wake in the morning, Maggie is still asleep. She's all curled up and looks like she did when she was a little girl. It amazes me how time seems to have flown. It feels like just a few years ago we were little, playing with dolls, but now here she is getting married and I'm probably going to grow into an old maid, alone until the day I die. Then Jack and I can finally be together again. She wakes while I'm getting ready for class. I bypass my jeans and go straight for sweatpants and an oversized sweatshirt. I pull my hair up into a messy bun, grab my backpack and stuff my laptop into it.

"You aren't going to have any breakfast?" Maggie asks. "I'm going to meet Hunter in about an hour. Do you want to join us?"

"No thanks. I'm going to be late for my class if I do. But maybe lunch?" I lie. Really, I don't want to eat breakfast because I want to save my calories for a good dinner. I've got to get rid of this paunchy belly. By lunch I'm starving and having a hard time concentrating, so I go to the cafeteria for a salad. As I eat, I start to feel like I might throw up. I look around to see if I know anyone there. I don't want to embarrass myself or gross anyone out, so I quickly leave, throwing my salad away on my way out.

The days until we leave for home are all some variation of the salad event. I get something to eat, can't stomach it and end up throwing it away.

I must have a stomach bug, I think, and hope.

Thanksgiving can't seem to come quick enough for me, but finally on Friday we're on our way home. Hunter and Maggie follow me in his car as I drive my car. They're planning on spending the first half of the week with us and then the second with his family so she can meet them. As we drive into Portland, I can't help thinking how lonely it's going to feel without Maggie there. It'll be the first Thanksgiving we've ever spent apart. It makes me feel sad.

When we pull into the driveway Mom and Scott come out to greet us. It feels so good to be embraced by Mom. She's always had a way of making me feel safe. I even give Scott a hug. He looks at me surprised but my only response is a smile. I'm not really sure why I gave him that hug. I think it's because I just really appreciate him watching over Mom.

I go to my room, drop my bags on the floor and fall into my own bed. I feel so exhausted. I hope that now I'm in a familiar place, the place where I've had most of my dreams of Jack, he might show up in them again. I can only hope.

That night at dinner Mom gives me a worried look when I don't eat very much. "I've got a bit of a stomach bug, that's all," I tell her. I don't want her to worry unnecessarily so I don't tell her how long it has been going on.

Once Hunter is settled and Scott leaves, I go to my bedroom and get ready for bed. I'm about to get into bed when I hear a soft knock on the door. "Come in," I say. The door opens and Mom comes in. She's got that worried look on her face that I can't stand. She comes in and sits with me on my bed.

"How are you doing, Jenn...really. And don't tell me it's just a flu bug," she says.

"What if it really is a flu bug?" I say starting to feel defensive. I really don't want to think about it or even imagine what might be happening with my body. She puts her hand on my leg and gives me that look that has shamed me my whole life, the look that says, "I love you and that's why I'm asking." I bow my head and look at my hands for a long time.

Finally, I look up at her and say, "I don't know Mom. I've felt like throwing up for about a week now. I can't eat much, and my stomach is all bloated. I can't even get into my jeans anymore." For a moment I think she's going to cry, but then she plasters on her brave face. The one that says that we'll figure things out, and whatever may come we'll face it together.

"I made an appointment with your GP, Dr. Powers for Monday at 11 a.m.," she reports. "We'll get this all figured out." I nod.

As she's about to get up, I grab her hand and say, "Thanks, Mom."

"Of course, Sweetheart," is her reply. She closes the door softly behind her. I lie in the darkness, staring at the moon through half parted blinds. It's a giant harvest moon and it's glowing so brilliantly. It's dazzling. As I watch the moon, I start to think about God. I wonder what he's like and if he understands what this earth life is like. I believe that he cares because he gave me Jack. I begin to feel ashamed that I sent him away when God had given him to me as a gift to help me through these trying times. I slide out of bed and kneel on the floor and pour out my heart to God, asking for his forgiveness for sending Jack away. I beg for Jack to come back. Peace washes over me, so I get back into bed fully expecting to dream of Jack tonight. But instead, I'm in the swing in the backyard with Dad again.

"Don't worry, Tiger, it won't be much longer until you can see him again," Dad says.

"But why can't I see him now?" I ask.

He grins at me and says with a tap on my nose, "You need to learn to be more patient. It's not time yet. That's why you can't see him."

Disappointed, I start to swing. He begins to swing alongside me. I speed up and so does he. It's turning into a contest to see who can go the highest. Soon he's got me laughing so hard I can hardly breathe. I slow to a stop, trying to catch my breath. I turn to him and say, "Thanks, Dad, for being here for me. It really means a lot to me."

"Sweetheart, it's time for me to go now. Just remember that you are loved by more people than you realize." He turns and starts to walk away but then stops. He looks at me and says, "I like Scott. He's good for your mother. Tell her I said to keep him around." He smiles and is gone, and I wake up. I look at the window, I can't see the moon anymore and it looks like the sun might be thinking about coming up. I look at my clock. Sure enough it's 6:30 and the first yawning stretches of sunlight are peeking over the horizon.

It's too early to get up, I think and pull my blanket up over my head and fall back to sleep.

At 8:00, I hear dance music playing in the kitchen. I get up and find Hunter and Maggie making pancakes while dancing around the kitchen. I watch through groggy eyes and smile. Mom comes up behind me and we watch enthralled. Maggie is wearing her baby doll pajamas again, and furry blue slippers on her feet. She's using the pancake turner as a microphone. Hunter is wearing pajama bottoms and a t-shirt. His hair is messy, but it looks good on him. He's using the empty egg carton as a guitar. They're rocking out so hard they don't even notice us until the song ends and we begin to clap. Hunter blushes and quickly puts the egg carton on the counter. Maggie of course bows and curtsies, enjoying the accolades.

Mom and I help with the rest of the breakfast preparations and before long we're all sitting down to eat. I eat an obligatory amount, fighting to keep it down, then go to my room to get ready for the day. I still can't fit into my jeans. I decide I need to look up what could be causing this. Most of the suggestions are obviously not the cause of the problem, but there are a few that seem more likely. The first on the list is irritable bowel syndrome or just plain constipation.

I have been constipated lately, I think, and decide to take a laxative or stool softener to see if that solves the problem.

That night I take a laxative and, in the morning, I'm feeling more normal, but it does nothing to reduce the bloat. Over the weekend I try other suggestions I read about on the internet. I exercise, stay away from carbs as much as possible and drink more water, but none of it seems to reduce the size of my belly.

On Monday, I go to my doctor's appointment. Dr. Powers examines my stomach. "Well, it could be a number of things. Your body has undergone a lot of trauma with the surgery and the chemo. It could just be your body trying to recalibrate itself. If you'd like, I can drain off that fluid," he says.

"Yes, please," I say. It takes a few minutes to get everything, including me, prepped for the procedure. He inserts a long needle into the side of my belly and begins to drain off the fluid.

"You're going to feel so much better once you get this all drained off," he says. Eight vials later I feel more like myself again.

"Thank you, Doctor," I say.

"If that fluid comes back, let me know," he says and sends me on my way.

Now that I can fit into my jeans again, I feel a lot better about everything. My stomach even feels better, and I feel like I'm going to be able to eat a little more and keep it down.

Maggie and Hunter leave on Wednesday to be with his family for the holiday. Mom and I stand in the open doorway and watch them drive away. It makes me feel so forlorn for both me and Mom.

"Scott's invited us to spend Thanksgiving with him and his family," Mom says. "You haven't met his kids yet, have you?"

"No, I haven't and to tell you the truth I haven't even thought that he might have kids," I say feeling rather dumb for not even considering it. We walk into the kitchen. "How many does he have?"

"He has two, all grown and one who's a senior in high school. The oldest is Tanner. He's married and lives in town. They're expecting their first baby in February. Then there's Shannon. She's the next oldest. She's working on a master's degree in marketing. She isn't married, but there is a boyfriend who could potentially become serious. Brock is the youngest. He graduates this spring. He says he's going to take a 'gap year' which I've heard is the new thing to do," she says.

"A gap year?" I ask. "Isn't that what Maggie did? She took a year off after graduation to work before going to college."

"Yeah, I guess you're right. Apparently, a lot of kids are taking that year off to work, travel, and do whatever to have a break from school," Mom explains.

"The year I graduated," I say, "some of my classmates did that, but they didn't call it a gap year. They just called it working, or traveling, or whatever. I guess calling it a gap year sounds more like a thoughtful decision instead of, 'I'm too poor to go to school yet or I'm just sick of school and want to see the world', " I say.

Thanksgiving is very different for me this year. We arrive at Scott's house with arm loads of pies. Pies are Mom's specialty. That's how Mom and Dad met. She'd made pie for a social they'd both attended and Dad, who had thought that pie making was a lost art, couldn't take his eyes off the beautiful blonde carrying a delicious pie that she had made from scratch. They started dating, falling in love quickly. A few short months later they got married. Now, she's dating Scott. I hope he appreciates Mom's pie talents as much as Dad did.

Scott introduces me to his kids. Tanner and his wife, Melissa are really nice. Shannon is a bit standoffish. I get the feeling she is sizing me up, for what I don't know. Brock is too busy playing video games with a friend to bother being introduced to me.

"Brock! We have company. It's time to turn that thing off and be social," Scott says.

"Kenny's here, Dad. I *am* being social," Brock says without even looking up or missing a shot of his game.

"That's not the kind of *social* I'm talking about. I'm talking about stopping your game, meeting our guests, joining in a conversation with them that's longer than five words, kind of social," he scolds.

"But Daaaad," Brock complains.

"Kenny," Scott says gently, putting his hand on Kenny's shoulder, "I think it's time for you to go home."

"Yes, Sir," Kenny says, looking very much afraid. He jumps up, dashes for the door grabbing his coat as he passes the place where he'd left it on the floor and is gone before Brock can say a word.

Brock slams the game controller on the coffee table, stands up, turns to me, and says, while holding up a finger for each word, "Hello," one finger up. "I'm," second finger up. "Brock," third. "So," finger. "Nice," finger. "To," finger. "Meet," finger. "You," finger. Then he turns to Scott and says, "There, Dad. That was eight whole words. Are you happy now?"

"That wasn't a conversation, Brock," Scott says.

With a snooty look, Brock says, "We spoke with our eyes." With that he storms from the room.

Scott turns to Mom and says, "I'm sorry about Brock, Sandy. As you can see, he has a lot of growing up to do."

Mom puts her hand on his arm and says, "That's alright. I've had my share of teenage problems with my girls. Thankfully they outgrew it." Mom winks at me, reminding me of all the times I got lippy with her.

I couldn't say I was disappointed that Brock didn't want to talk to me. I'm sure we don't have anything in common. It would have just been so awkward.

After a while of uncomfortable conversation with Shannon, the turkey is done, the food is placed on the table and we sit down to eat. Without anything being said, Brock makes his appearance, sitting next to me. He feels all prickly and surly but to my surprise he actually tries to make conversation.

"My dad says you're going to college," he says.

"Yes, I am," I say as I pass him the peas.

"Whatcha majoring in?"

"I haven't decided yet. I've mainly been working on my gen ed classes."

"Me and Kenny are gonna backpack across Europe next year," Brock says.

"Really. That sounds interesting."

"Yeah, it's going to be totally dope!" he says.

"I'm sure it will be...dope," I say, feeling very uncomfortable with the conversation.

"Hey," Brock says, pointing at me. "You should totally come with us."

"That's very nice of you to invite me, Brock, but I'm afraid I won't be able to."

"What, you got a boyfriend or something?"

"Yes, something like that."

"Oh," he says and thankfully, turns his attention to his meal. The rest of the meal is passed in silence between Brock and me. Mom chats amiably with Scott's older children while I feel as if I've been relegated to the kid's table. As soon as dinner is over Brock retreats to his room again, leaving the rest of us to play board games and eat pie on our own. A couple of hours later Brock emerges, grabs a dinner plate, loads it with multiple pieces of pie, drowns it in whipping cream and returns to his room. That's the last time I ever lay eyes on Brock.

Chapter 16 Forgiveness

As nice as having time off is, I'm glad when Thanksgiving vacation comes to an end. I'm a little worried about finals and just the whole Thanksgiving without Maggie made it feel too strange. She assures me that next year she and Hunter will spend it with us. It's weird having to share my sister with people I've never met, but I guess it's all part of growing up. I drive back to school by myself. I'm hoping Maggie will be there when I arrive, but she doesn't make it back until almost midnight. She's exhausted, but happy. I'm glad it went well for her. I want to hear all about it, but it's late and we both have class in the morning, so it'll have to wait.

The next evening Maggie tells me about her visit with Hunter's family. "Did you know that Hunter has seven siblings?! He has six sisters and one brother!" Maggie exclaims.

"Really?" I say. "Where is he in the family?"

"He's the third. He has two older sisters. They're both married with a couple kids each. They were so cute, but noisy. That'll take some getting used to. Anyway, his brother is just younger than him by a couple of years. He's going to a college in California. This is his first semester. Then there's Abigail, she's a senior in high school, is a cheerleader and still gets straight A's. I could never have done all that. The best grades I got were Bs and Cs, and I wasn't even a cheerleader," Maggie says.

"It also depends on what classes she's taking. You took some pretty hard classes your senior year," I say. She looks doubtful and changes the subject.

"Oh, and Charlie's a sophomore, Lexi's in eighth grade and Mariah's in sixth."

"Wow!" was all I was able to get out before she continues.

"His parents are so nice, too. It'll be so nice to have a dad. I've never really experienced that." Her statement kind of shocks me. I'd never really thought about how it was for her, not having a dad around. I feel sad for her, but I am glad she's finally going to have one in her life.

"While we were there, we talked about wedding dates. We're thinking of June 5th. The semester will be over and that will give us several months to get everything ready," she says.

"Wow! That's really fast!" I say.

"I know, but his parents are very religious, and they believe that having a long engagement is only asking for trouble," she explains.

"I guess it would cut down on complications," I say thoughtfully. "Well, I'll do whatever you need me to do to get ready for the wedding."

She gives me a hug and says, "I know you will."

"I have to admit something though," I say.

"What is it?" Maggie asks.

"Hunter showed me your ring the night before you got engaged and he told me how he was planning to pop the question," I confess. Maggie gets an uncomfortable look on her face.

"Since we're being totally honest. I have something to confess. I've been wanting to tell you this for months now, but it never seemed to work out," she says. Her face is a mix of guilt and fear.

"What is it?" I say feeling concerned.

"Well, you know when Hunter first came to visit?"

"Yeah."

"And we went for that hike?"

"Yeah."

"Well, we…" she mumbled so softly I couldn't hear what she said.

"You did what?"

She sighs heavily and says, "Hunter and I kissed." She puts her hands on her face in shame.

"You KISSED!?"

"Jenn, I'm sorry, but it gets worse."

"It gets WORSE? And how might THAT be?" I ask angrily.

She's in agony. "We started texting each other right after that. Jenn, I'm really sorry."

"WHAT!!!" I shout as I shoot up off my bed. I start pacing the room feeling betrayed. "MAGGIE, how could you?"

"I know Jenn, I'm a horrible person and I'm really sorry," she says looking miserable. She cowers on her bed like a stricken dog. I suddenly feel sorry for her and very confused about how I feel about this revelation.

"I'm going for a walk," I announce and grab my coat on my way out the door.

I wander campus aimlessly. I pass Jill and Nate outside of the library. Jill comes up and shows me the ring Nate had given her when he proposed. I congratulate them and go into the library to get warm. I go to my favorite study spot and sit to think. It's a secluded corner with three dark brown, overstuffed chairs gathered around a small, squat table.

I curl up in one of the chairs, sinking into its comforting depths and chew on my thumbnail, wondering, *Should I be mad? To be honest, I really wasn't that invested in Hunter anyway but at the same time they did betray my trust.* As I think about this the anger rears its ugly head again. I stand up to pace some more when my eyes land on the painting on the wall above my chair, the one I'd looked at hundreds of times before. This time, though, I recognize it. It's Jack's ship, the painting that Mr. Williams was painting. I draw closer to it to examine it. I run my fingers along the signature. "J. Williams," it says. I swallow hard and my heart longs to be on that ship with Jack. All my anger toward Maggie and Hunter fades away leaving my heart full of Jack. I know I can no longer be angry with them. Something inside me knows they were always meant to be together. I was just meant to introduce them.

As I head back to our dorm I think, *I can't just let this go entirely. Maggie really needs to pay some kind of penance.* As I near our hall I finally come up with a plan.

"Ok, Maggie," I say as I walk into our room, "Here's the deal." Maggie looks at me with wide eyes and nods. "You two did me wrong," I say.

Maggie puts her head in her hands and says, "I know. I know. I'm so sorry."

"You know I have every right to be mad at you, but I just can't be," I say. She sighs with relief and goes to hug me, but I stop her.

"I'm not done yet," I say. She sits back and looks at me with wide eyes. "I feel that you owe me something, and I have something very special in mind." She scrunches up her lips and narrows her eyes. From experience, she knows I plan to have her do something she isn't going to like.

"Ok, what is it?" she says hesitantly.

"You rub my feet every day for a week for at least ten minutes and this whole betrayal will be forgotten," I say.

At first, she looks as if she's going to protest but then stops herself and asks, "Socks on or off?"

"Socks off and with lotion," I say.

"Uhg," she groans, her shoulders slumping. "Jenn, you know how much I hate touching other people's feet, especially with lotion," she whines.

"Well, it's this or I'll have to be mad at you," I say.

She rolls her eyes and finally consents. "For only a week – Monday through Friday," she says.

"No way! Seven whole days. A day for each of Hunter's siblings," I say lifting my eyebrows and smirking.

"You're evil, Jenn, you know that? Fine, I'll do it. When do I start?"

"Right now," I say, taking off my shoes and socks, and putting my feet in Maggie's lap. She fakes a gag, but then gets to work.

Chapter 17 *Phyllis Works Miracles*

There are just three weeks until we go home for Christmas. We have finals, packing up and then we'll be heading home. Thankfully, once we get home, we'll have a week to shop before Christmas. I haven't spent any time even thinking about what to give anyone for Christmas.

As Christmas draws nearer, I start to notice that my stomach is getting big again. I'd hoped I wouldn't have to wear my sweats to class anymore, but it looks like I'll have to.

The day of my English final Fatima and I go to the lounge to say our goodbyes.

"Thank you, Fatima, for all your help this semester," I say, giving her a hug.

"It was my pleasure, Jennifer," she says.

"We'll have to get together next semester," I say. "Maybe we could take another class together."

"Perhaps," she says with a sad smile. "I suspect you will be very busy this next semester."

"You're probably right. Knowing Maggie, she'll have me working my tail off helping her get ready for the wedding," I say.

"That is not what I was referring to, but in time you will know," she says. A shiver of fear dances through me when she says this.

When our finals are done, Maggie and I drive home. Hunter goes to his parents' house in California. He'll come to Portland in a week and spend the remainder of the holiday with us.

As I'm unpacking my suitcase, I pull out my jeans and look at them closely. I hold them up to my waist and see that they're not going to fit. It's discouraging. I fold them and put them in the drawer, deciding I better go back to the doctor. I need to find out why I'm bloating so much.

I spend the week shopping for Christmas and squeeze in a trip to my GP. Dr. Powers examines my belly again. This time he doesn't seem so sure that it's just my body readjusting itself. He schedules me for another endoscopy.

Here we go again, I think.

As I'm being prepped for the exam, Scott comes into the room. He's not doing the endoscopy this time because he's dating Mom and it would be a conflict of interest. But he still wants to be there to support us through it.

When the procedure is over, I start to wake up as they're wheeling me to the recovery room. I watch the ceiling as the lights flash by, one after the other. I look around and see images sliding by in a blur. My nose starts to itch so I reach up to scratch it. I have an IV in the back of my hand and the movement of the gurney makes it hard to control my arm. I overshoot my nose and hit myself in the cheek instead. I try again. This time I'm successful. I look around again and see Jack walking alongside my gurney...at least I think it's him.

"Jack?" I whisper. He turns, smiles at me and winks. "I knew you would come," I say and reach out to touch his hand but he's too far away.

We finally come to a stop. They park me in an alcove similar to the one they prepped me in. Jack leans up against the wall.

The nurse touches my arm to get my attention, and says with a smile, "Your mom and sister will be in shortly." I nod and look back toward Jack. Before long, Mom and Maggie are by my side, but Scott isn't with them.

"Where's Scott?" I croak.

"He went to look at the scans and talk to the doctor," Mom says. "How're you feeling?"

"Just peachy," I say. "Mom, Jack's here." She looks around the room.

"Where, Honey? I don't see him," she says. I look to where I'd seen him standing, but now that I'm feeling more awake, I don't see him anymore. It makes me sad.

When Scott comes in, he's carrying the films of my scans and looking like he might be sick. Mom gives him a questioning look. He just shakes his head. I hear a stifled sob from Mom. He doesn't have to say a word, I know exactly what he's going to say.

He looks at me on the gurney. "Hey there," he says with a smile. "How're you feeling?"

I don't feel like mincing words, so I blurt out, "How much longer do I have?"

He looks at Mom, clears his throat and says, "One or two months."

"What?" Maggie cries. "Jenn, you can't leave me! You're supposed to be my maid of honor."

"Sorry, I'm going to ruin your wedding, Maggie, but I don't seem to have much choice in the matter," I say.

"No, you have to be there," she cries. "We'll just have to get married next week."

Mom puts her hand on Maggie's arm and says, "I don't think we can put a wedding together that fast, Sweetheart."

Maggie turns to Mom and says, "I don't care about the dress, the cake or any of it. The only thing I care about is for Jenn to be there with us. We'll get married at City Hall if we have to. We're getting married next week!" She says it with such finality that no one dares question her. I look at Mom and see how distraught she is about all this and realize something.

"Maggie," I begin, "Mom has been dreaming of our wedding days for a long time. She wants it to be special."

Maggie looks at Mom and realizes that she would be depriving our mother of something she's dreamed about as long as Maggie has been alive. She thinks for a while then says, "Ok, how about Hunter and I get married next week and then have a renewal of vows with the dress, cake, and all of that, during the summer?" Mom thinks this over and nods her agreement.

As I'm getting dressed, Maggie goes outside to call Hunter. When we get to the car, Maggie's still talking to Hunter, and she's been crying. I hate that I'm the cause of all this trauma. I wish it was different. I wish I could change things, but it's impossible.

The ride home is a quiet one, and when we get there, I immediately go to my room. I can feel Mom's and Maggie's eyes following me. I want to turn and yell at them to stop looking at me, but I don't because this isn't their fault and I know they're suffering just as much as I am. I lie on my bed and stare up at the ceiling not knowing what to do. I feel numb inside. I can't even cry. I guess I'm just in shock. As I look up at the ceiling, I hear a gentle whisper. I can't quite understand what it's saying so I decide it must just be the sound of some machinery or the pipes that are resembling the sound of a whisper.

After a long while I decide I don't want to spend my last days on this earth lying around in my room. I want to see friends and family – maybe even do some things I've always wanted to do before I get too sick to do anything. First order of business – take an active part in Maggie's wedding. I come out of my room and see Mom holding onto Maggie as she cries. Actually, I think they're both crying. I sit down on the couch with them, and we hug each other so closely we can hardly breathe.

After a while, I let go, clap my hands together and announce, "Enough of this blubbering, we have a wedding to plan." Maggie and Mom laugh through their tears. I grab a piece of paper and a pencil.

"Ok, what do we need?" I ask. We discuss possible venues, refreshments, who to officiate, who to invite, and the list goes on. Once we've got our list, we brainstorm how to make it all happen.

"Phyllis, next door, used to be a wedding planner. I'm going to call her for some help," Mom says.

"Good idea," I say. "I can put together invitations and have them printed. If we use same day service at the store, we can have them ready right away. Then Maggie can take them to her closest friends and call our nearest relatives." Our plan seems to be coming together. Mom calls our next-door neighbor, Phyllis. She's more than happy to help, especially when she learns the reason why we're having it next week.

She comes over immediately and sits down with Maggie to get an idea of what she wants for the wedding. After a couple of hours together, Phyllis's notebook is full. As she's walking out the door she says, "Now, Sandy, I don't want you to worry about a thing. I've got everything under control. I'll take care of everything. You just enjoy your girls."

"Oh," Maggie says, suddenly thinking of something more. "What about the invitations?"

Phyllis just smiles, pats her notebook, and says, "I've got it all right here, even the invitations. Don't you worry about a single thing. I've got it all under control." And then she's gone like an angel in the night.

Hunter and his mom fly into town the day after Christmas to help with preparations and to be a support to our family. Maggie was right, Hunter's mom is very sweet. The moment she first meets me, she hugs me so tight I can hardly breathe. Then she kisses me on the cheek.

The only thing Phyllis left for us to do is figure out the wedding dress. We go to several stores, but Maggie can't seem to find one she loves. We return home feeling tired and discouraged. Mom disappears for a while. We all figure she's gone to lie down until she comes into the room carrying a large white box.

She sets it down in front of Maggie. "Mom, is this what I think it is?" Maggie asks.

"I don't know. What do you think it is?" Mom says.

"Is this your wedding dress?"

Mom grins shyly and says, "Yes. I thought it might give you some inspiration to find the one that suits you." Maggie gently pulls the top off the box. On top is a white, brimmed hat with a veil cascading down the back. I move closer to get a better look. Maggie puts the hat on. Of course it looks good on her, but it is definitely a blast from the past. She then pulls out a white, silk dress. The bodice is pleated, wraps around and ties in a bow on the side. There's a little skirt thing attached to the bodice that's short in the front and grows longer as it moves around the back.

"What's this?" Maggie asks, holding out the skirt thing.

"It's called a peplum. It was fashionable back in the early '90's," she says, seeming a little embarrassed by her fashion choices back then.

"I love it!" Maggie exclaims. The sleeves have a slight poof at the top then taper down to a point on the back of the hands. The skirt is floor length and straight and, in the back, it flares out nicely into a short train. The whole dress is tastefully embellished with white flourishes and small pearls.

"Mom, it's beautiful," Maggie gasps. "I'm going to go try it on." She takes the dress to her room and after a short while she comes back, looking like a bride.

"Wow!" Mom says. "I don't think I looked that good in it."

Hunter whistles. He hands her the hat, and she goes to the bathroom to look at herself. She comes back beaming and we all know what she's going to say.

"This is the one," she says. "I want this to be my wedding dress. Except for the hat.   I want a traditional veil with a tiara." Mom is smiling so big I'm afraid her face might crack.   It fills me with joy.

The morning of the wedding, I wake feeling tired and weak. I know I've done more these last few days than I should have. Now I'm worried I'm not going to have the strength to last the entire day. I struggle just to get out of bed. When I stand, I feel dizzy. I sway precariously until the dizziness passes. It feels like it's going to take more strength than I have just to make it to the bathroom. I take one step then plop back down on my bed. "Nooo!" I growl in frustration. This is not how this day is supposed to play out. I'm near panic when I remember the other times when I've prayed and received answers. I decide it's time to pray again. I slide uncontrollably to the floor and land hard on my knees. I lean on the bed for support and pray for strength both physically and emotionally. I feel Dad standing near me. I turn and look; I don't see him, but I do feel his strength. I feel as if I'm being lifted by some unseen person. I get to my feet and am able to dress myself. I slip into the burgundy bridesmaid dress Phyllis brought over for me. I look at the shoes I'd planned to wear with my dress, but don't feel I could safely manage the heels, so I opt for a pair of black flats. Phyllis has arranged to have some of the cute teenage girls in the neighborhood come and do our makeup and hair. I'm grateful for that because I don't think I can do it by myself.

I hear a soft knock on my door. It's Lizzy, the teenage girl from across the street. "Phyllis asked me to come in and check on you," she says. "Is there anything I can do for you?" I realize if I'm going to take part in this wedding, I'm going to have to swallow my pride and accept help.

"Yes, could you help me into the bathroom to brush my teeth?" She cheerfully comes to my side, puts a supporting arm around me, and guides me to the bathroom. When I'm done, she helps me out to the dining room where the girls have makeup, mirrors, brushes, combs, curling irons, flat irons, and tons of bobby pins, clips, and ribbon. I sit down and Kayla, the girl I used to babysit when I was in middle school, starts to work on me. Her style seems to be similar to mine, so I trust her judgment in doing my hair and makeup. A few minutes later, Maggie, Mom, and Hunter's mom join me. We chat and laugh as the girls work their wonder on us. I lose track of time. I'm not sure how long it's been once they finish, but what I do know is that we all look fabulous, especially Maggie. She looks like a princess. She excuses herself to go and get dressed. Mom goes with her. I want to, but I don't have the strength. I watch them go, but then Lizzy is at my side.

"Maggie needs her sister right now," she says, helping me to my feet. Gratefully, I take her hand. I've regained some of my strength, but I'm still not confident in it. She helps me walk into the bedroom, sets me on the bed and leaves. I watch as Mom helps Maggie put on the wedding dress without messing up her hair or makeup. It *is* good to be with them, especially since my days are numbered. I catch a glimpse of myself in the mirror and it shocks me, because I've never thought I was very pretty – Maggie is the true beauty of the family. But, as I study my reflection in the mirror, I realize I look like one of those super thin models whose bones can be seen through the fabric of their clothing. Kayla did such a good job bringing out what natural beauty I have.

When Maggie is dressed and ready to go, we walk out and find that the girls and all their paraphernalia are gone, except Lizzy. She's waiting outside the bedroom door to help me. We go to the living room and find Jeff, the neighbor from a few houses down, waiting for us. He bows and says, "I'm going to be your chauffeur today." He extends his arm to Maggie and walks her to a waiting limousine. It's black and sleek. We follow her into the vehicle. None of us have ever ridden in a limousine before. Phyllis has thought of everything.

Jeff drives us to one of the fanciest houses in the neighborhood. He pulls up in front, helps us out and escorts us into the house. Phyllis is there in the entryway waiting for us. She leads us to one of the rooms on the main floor where we wait. After some time, she comes and gets us.

She leads us toward the back of the house where there's a large game room that's been cleared of the gaming equipment and turned into a magical wonderland. Plants, ribbons, lace, and rolls of mesh have sprouted all around the room. At the far end is the officiant and next to him is Hunter, looking all dazzling in his black tuxedo. Hunter's dad waits by the door to the wedding wonderland, to escort Maggie to the front and present her to his son. Maggie beams when she sees him, leans in, and gives her new father a kiss on the cheek. He grins and the wedding march begins. The audience rises. The room is full of friends, family, and neighbors. So many people have come to show their love and support. My eyes fill with tears. I want to weep for the love I feel in this room.

As we reach the front, Mom sits in the chair designated for the mother of the bride. It's positioned in a way to give her an optimal view of her daughter. Maggie hands me her bouquet and we get into position. I sway for a moment and then I see someone has placed a stool next to me. I sit on it with a sigh. And the wedding begins.

The officiant steps forward and says, "Welcome, everyone to the union of Magnolia May Cooper..." I see Maggie cringe when he says her full given name. She's never liked it, but now everyone in the neighborhood knows what it is. "...and Hunter Wayne Johnson. They would like to thank all of you for being here to share in this special day with them. You may now be seated." There's a rustling of fabric and chairs as the audience sits.

"Friends and family, we're all here to encourage Hunter and Magnolia as they join their lives together as husband and wife. This union is a new creation, one bonded by love. This love is the mortar that will hold the two of you together, especially when times get tough. During those times, remember to cling to each other. Turn to each other for guidance, understanding and forgiveness. As you enter into married life, remember what you love about each other this day. Reflect on those things regularly and add to the list as the years progress. Remember that all strong and lasting marriages are built on love, trust, and respect."

I look at Mom and see her wiping tears from her cheek. It warms my heart.

The officiant turns to the bride and groom in turn and says, "Hunter, Magnolia." Each time the officiant says her name I hear Maggie grind her teeth. "Cherish one another. Make it a habit to always do the little things that show love, respect, and trust. It's the little things, the little kindnesses and tender moments that should be the rule for your actions, not the exception. Remember that you're on the same team – Team Johnson." This elicits a soft chuckle from the audience. Hunter takes this opportunity to lean forward and whisper something to the officiant. He nods and continues, "Together you can fight whatever demons, and defeat any enemies that may come your way. As you build a life together, forge bonds that can never be broken, neither here on earth nor in heaven above. If you do this, you will experience heaven on earth."

The officiant smiles and turns to Hunter and says, "Now, Hunter, do you, of your own free will, take Magnolia May Cooper as your lawfully wedded wife to love, protect, and defend—as long as you both shall live?

Hunter's grin is exuberant when he says, "I do."

"Now, *Maggie*," he says with a wink. Hunter must have told him to call her Maggie, "do you, of your own free will, take Hunter Wayne Johnson, as your lawfully wedded husband to love, protect, and defend—as long as you both shall live?"

All eyes are on Maggie. She grins and says with surety, "I do."

The officiant says, "Very good. Now who has the rings?" A cute little boy steps forward carrying a pillow with the wedding rings tied to it. His mother, who's a prettier version of Hunter, no doubt his sister, unties the ribbons and hands the rings to the officiant, who bends down and ruffles the little boy's hair.

The officiant then hands Hunter Maggie's ring and says, "Do you Hunter Wayne Johnson, vow to place Magnolia May Cooper above all else, before all others, and stand true and unmovable in your support for her through the good and the bad?"

Hunter looks Maggie in the eyes and vows emphatically, "I will". He then gently slips the ring onto Maggie's finger.

The officiant then looks at Maggie and repeats what he said to Hunter to which she answers with a resounding, "I will." She in turn slips Hunter's ring on his finger.

"By the power vested in me by the State of Oregon and God, I now pronounce you, husband and wife," the officiant says. "You may now kiss for the first time as a married…." The officiant doesn't even get a chance to finish the sentence when Maggie lunges at Hunter and kisses him with such joy and passion it makes me blush. Everyone laughs.

To the audience the officiant says, "Let me introduce to you Mr. and Mrs. Hunter and Magno… Maggie Johnson. Please rise and congratulate the new couple." Everyone stands and cheers.

In the blink of an eye the room is transformed and readied for the reception. The floor is hardwood and perfect for dancing. Phyllis approaches me and says, "I've got a special place for you." She leads me to an overstuffed armchair that's been placed on the edge of all the action. I sit down with a plop. Someone pushes a button, and the footrest rises into position to make me comfortable. This chair is so comfortable I might just fall asleep, but I won't because I don't want to miss anything.

The party continues even after Maggie and Hunter leave for their honeymoon. His parents booked them a weekend getaway to Las Vegas. Maggie has never been there and is excited for the experience. Someone handed her a one-hundred-dollar bill with the instructions to blow it gambling. Maggie laughed but knowing her she's going to stash it away for a rainy day.

When they're gone, I call Lizzy over and ask her to take me home. She happily agrees. Jeff is still at the reception, so he drives Lizzy and me to my house. Lizzy chats the whole way about the wedding and the reception. It's fun to listen to her version of the events. When we get to the house, she helps me to my room and then leaves. I struggle out of the bridesmaid dress and into my pajamas. I don't have the strength to wash my face so I just accept the fact that in the morning my pillow will look like a Picasso version of my face. I lie in my bed and as I start to drift off, I hear the whispers again. This time though, I can tell it really is a voice. I still can't quite understand what it is saying, but it feels like it's calling to me.

Chapter 18 When Darkness Falls

The following Monday, Maggie and Hunter return and take up residence in Maggie's room. While they were gone Mom replaced Maggie's old twin bed with a queen to accommodate the newlyweds.

It's good to see them. The house felt so lonely while they were gone. I spend most of my time these days watching movies and TV. My weakened state doesn't allow me the strength to do much of anything else. A hospice nurse comes in every other day to help take care of me. Mom wants me to be in a central place so I'm not alone in my room all day with only an occasional visitor. So a hospital bed is brought in and placed in the corner of the family room, which has now been designated as my space. The mattress of the hospital bed is as hard as a rock, which is very uncomfortable for my now bony frame. With a gift card they'd received Maggie and Hunter buy me a nice foam pad to make me more comfortable.

Mom tries to stay positive and cheerful, but I can hear her crying at night. I hate that I bring her such sadness. As word gets around about my imminent demise, more visitors come to say goodbye to me. Friends from high school come and sing to me. My aunts and uncles come for a few days as well as some of my cousins. Neighbors come too.

I've lost track of what day it is and how long it's been since the wedding. One day the doorbell rings. Maggie runs to get it. I hear her talking to someone. The voice is female and familiar, but I don't have the energy to try to figure out who it is. After a few minutes, Maggie ushers back Lizzy's mom, Helen Masterson from across the street. At first, I want to send her away, but when I catch a glimpse of her peeking around the door, I decide to let her stay. Her smile is warm, and her blonde hair looks like a halo around her plump face. Something about her presence brings me peace.

"Thank you for coming," I say as she makes herself comfortable in the chair next to my bed.

"You've been on my mind all week and I felt I should come over. Here," she says as she hands me a bouquet of flowers. "I thought these might brighten your day." I take them and hold them to my nose. Their sweet aroma fills me with memories of summer adventures with Maggie when we were young.

I smile and hand them to Maggie who puts them in a vase, "Thank you. They're beautiful."

"I got them while I was out shopping. I thought of you when I saw them and just had to get them for you," she says. "I also brought a poem I want to share with you. Do you mind if I read it to you?"

"No, I don't mind. Go ahead."

She holds up a picture of a young, bald boy around five years old wearing superman pajamas and funny glasses with a bulbous nose attached to them. Above the picture is the boy's name, his birthdate and…. death date. Underneath is a poem called *Heaven's Light*. Mrs. Masterson clears her throat and says, "This is my son, Peter. He died several years ago from cancer when he was just five years old. This poem brought me a lot of hope and comfort during that time of darkness and despair. I hope it will for you as well. She clears her throat again and begins reading:

<u>Heaven's Light</u>
When darkness falls,
And death appears,
People often fear.
But could you see,
Beyond the veil,
You would gladly cheer.
For standing just,
Outside our view,
Wait our loved ones dear.
There's beauty there,
Just out of sight.

You will see it clear.
That when this life,
Comes to an end,
Heaven's light appears.

When she finishes, I sit quietly, contemplating these new ideas about death. I'd never considered that death just might be a good thing and maybe even desirable. We sit silently a few moments longer until Mrs. Masterson hesitantly says, "I hope I didn't upset you with this poem."

"No," I say adamantly. "It's just I've never thought of death in that way. It adds a whole new perspective to dying."

She smiles and says, "I'm glad it could help you." She turns and sees Mom standing behind her listening and asks, "Do you have any dishes or laundry I can do for you before I go?"

Mom smiles and says, "Thank you, but we can do them."

"No, I insist," Mrs. Masterson says. "In difficult times it helps to have a little extra help. It would be a privilege for me to help you."

Mom smiles, a tear in her eye, and whispers, "Thank you." Mrs. Masterson rises and follows Mom into the kitchen. I hear water running and dishes clattering. I stare out the window as I contemplate the poem she shared and the new possibilities it brings into existence for me.

I read the poem again and then a third time. "Could it be that death isn't all that bad?" I wonder. "I'd always believed that death was painful, horrible and something to actively prevent. Could it be a beautiful thing?" I remember when Dad was dying, there were times when he would stare off into an empty corner of the room and have what seemed like a conversation. As a kid, I thought he was going crazy, or the medicine was making him hallucinate. But now, I think that possibly there was someone who loved him there, helping him. I think about Jack. Oh how I miss him and wish I could ask him these questions, after all he *is* an expert on death. Then a thought dances across my mind. I wonder if Dad is with me now. Just then I feel him standing next to me. It fills me with warmth and love.

"Thank you, Daddy, and I love you." A tear slips down my cheek, but I quickly wipe it away when I hear footsteps close by.

Mrs. Masterson stops to say goodbye and promises to come by again. Mom walks her to the door. They talk for a few minutes. I see them embrace and Mom closes the door. Mom comes in and sits on the edge of the bed. "That was very nice of Helen to stop by," she says.

"Mom, do you think what that poem says is true?" I ask.

She takes my hand and with a gentle squeeze says, "I'd like to think so."

"I think Dad is here with us now."

She smiles sadly and wiggles into bed next to me. Taking my hand, she holds it against her heart and says, "I feel your father with me every single day."

"You do?"

"Yes...that's how I make it through each day."

"And now you have Scott too?"

"Scott? What do you mean?"

"Dad likes him."

She laughs lightly. "How do you know he likes him?"

"Because he came to me in a dream and told me. He thinks he's good for you."

"What?"

"I think Dad would be good with you marrying him."

We lie there silently for several moments, both deep in our own thoughts. "Mom," I say, tears sliding down my cheeks, "I miss Jack."

"I know you do, Sweetheart."

"Do you think he'll be there when I…you know, die."

"I don't know, but I do know he loves you and would never leave you alone. In fact, I wouldn't be surprised if he is here right now chatting it up with your dad." The thought of it makes me smile.

That night as I lie in the darkness, I hear the whispers again. I can understand them now. They're telling me that all will be well and they're looking forward to seeing me again. One of the voices sounds like my Grandma Cooper. Once again, I feel as if Dad is by my side. The comfort of it lulls me to sleep.

I'm sitting in the swing in our backyard again. Spring flowers are blossoming in a burgeoning flower bed and birds are chirping happily in the trees. Dad is sitting in the swing next to me.

"Hi there again," he says, and he begins to swing.

"Hi, Dad," I say.

"What was it like to die?" I ask.

He drags his feet on the ground and comes to a stop. He looks at me and says, "Well, I was in a lot of pain for a while, but the hospice staff were good about making sure I had a lot of morphine to ease the pain. The actual dying part wasn't so bad. Actually, it was rather easy. One moment I was in pain then the next I was pain free and able to move around freely."

"I'm sorry I wasn't there with you when you died."

"Don't worry about it. I wasn't alone. My grandparents were with me the whole time."

"I saw you talking to someone before you died, but no one was there."

"No one that you could see, yes, but I could see them. It was Grandpa Joe and Grandma Geraldine. They were preparing me to die."

"Really? I'm scared. How will I know when it's time?"

"I'll be there with you. When you see my hand, just grab a hold of it. The rest will be easy."

"Thank you. Oh, and what about Jack? When will I get to be with him?"

"Be patient, my dear. When it is time, he will be there."

"Please tell him I'm sorry and that I...I..." my voice gets caught on a sob, "I...love him." Admitting this aloud makes my heart ache. I wipe at the tears running down my cheeks. I look at Dad. He's smiling that all knowing smile of his and says with a wink, "He already knows." As he turns to leave, he says, "Remember, look for my hand." I nod and he's gone.

The next day is cloudy and dark. I wake to the sound of thunder and look at the window. Rain begins to pelt the glass and once more I'm struck with the realization that only a thin piece of glass is what protects us from the storm outside.

"Mom," I try yelling, no answer. I try again mustering all my strength, "Mom!" This time she hears me and comes running.

"WHAT!! What do you need?" she asks breathlessly, worry and fear colliding across her face.

"I didn't mean to scare you," I whisper. "It's just I want to go outside and feel the rain on my face one more time."

Maggie and Hunter come and help me out of bed. With them on either side of me they practically carry me outside. The rain is cold, and my skin is so tender that it feels almost like I'm being shot with airsoft pellets. *But I want this,* I remind myself. The three of us stand in the rain, faces lifted to the sky memorizing the feeling. After a few minutes I begin to shiver, and they take me in. Mom has a warm blanket ready for me. She wraps me in it like she did when I was little.

Each day I grow weaker. I can feel that the end is near, but it's still not time yet. I wish I could speed up this process. I want to just get it over with. Family members both living, and dead come to visit me. It feels as if my little space in the family room has a revolving door.

I'm not in any real pain, it's just that I can't eat, and my insides feel like they're one solid mass, which very well could be. I lie in my bed with my eyes closed because it takes too much energy to keep them open. I listen as Maggie and Hunter quietly talk. I try to move, but I'm too tired, too weak – in fact, I'm even too tired to breathe – and then it happens, I see Dad. He's holding out his hand and I take it. It's just that easy. It's like slipping out of my favorite pair of jeans.

I realize I'm no longer tired and weak – in fact, as I let go of Dad's hand, I freely float up near the ceiling like a helium balloon. I laugh and look down at Maggie and Hunter. She has her legs draped over his and they're huddled close together, talking quietly. They're so engrossed in their conversation they haven't even noticed I've died. I watch as Maggie tilts her face up to his, tears glistening on her cheeks. Hunter softly brushes them away with his thumbs. He leans in and gently kisses each of her eyes, her nose, and then, tenderly and sweetly kisses her lips. The sight of them and how perfectly they seem to fit together fills me with so much joy. Then I think of Mom and suddenly I'm there above her. She's in the kitchen and Scott has his arms around her. His broad hands caress her arm. I see him incline his head and kiss her forehead. A glow radiates from them, and I'm filled with the sense that I'm leaving my family in good hands.

I watch them for a few minutes, then I hear my name. I turn and Dad's next to me. "Are you ready to go, Tiger?" he asks. I look back at Mom and Scott one more time. I don't want to leave them, but Dad assures me that we can come to visit. I take his hand again and allow him to lead me. We move upwards and suddenly my home transforms into a dark tunnel. I'm a little scared, so I grasp tighter to Dad's hand. We walk in the darkness for a while, then we stop, and he says, "When darkness falls…" We take a couple of steps forward and pass through what feels like liquid fabric. Not only does it pass around me, but also through me and with a grin Dad finishes what he started to say, "…Heaven's light appears." We emerge into a place full of light, color, and beauty. I'm filled with an exquisite, peaceful feeling. This place seems as if it's made entirely of love.

I hear my name, "Jennifer." No one needs to tell me who it is. My heart already knows. I run to Jack and leap into his arms. He laughs, swinging me around as I squeal. When he sets me down, he kisses me long and slow. Our lips part and he says, "I love you so much."

I hug him and say, "I love you too." I feel as if my heart could burst for the love and gratitude I feel for this man. I know that if it weren't for him, my illness and death would have been much harder. He filled it with love, adventure, and helped me to live while I was dying. Over Jack's shoulder I see Dad watch us for a moment, smiling. Jack looks down at me and asks, "Are you ready for a tour of heaven?"

"I've already found heaven right here in your arms," I say, "and I intend to never be parted from you again."

Clara Matson, a Southern Nevada native, now lives in Idaho because it's much cooler. She's been creating and writing since a kid. She's a sister to seven, mother to three, aunt to (She lost count at about forty), and grandmother to one (the cutest of them all).

Clara has many books she's planning to write with more ideas coming to her daily. So don't get too comfortable with just this one book. There are many more to come.

You can follow her on Facebook:
https://www.facebook.com/Clara-Matson-Author-100449532727962